BREAKING POINT

OTHER BOOKS BY JAMES GUNN

BREAKING POINT

BY
JAMES GUNN

WALKER AND COMPANY
New York

C 1

First published in the United States of America in 1972 by the Walker Publishing Company, Inc.

Published simultaneously in Canada by Fitzhenry & Whiteside, Limited, Toronto.

ISBN: 0-8027-5552-6

Library of Congress Catalog Card Number: 72-80728

Printed in the United States of America.

ACKNOWLEDGEMENTS

"Breaking Point." Originally published in *Space Science Fiction*, March 1953.

"A Monster Named Smith." Originally published in *If*, July 1954.

"Cinderella Story." Originally published as "When the Shoe Fits" in *Vanguard Science Fiction*, June 1958.

"Teddy Bear." Originally published in *Worlds of Fantasy*, Issue 2, 1970.

"The Man Who Owned Tomorrow." Originally published in *Argosy*, July 1953.

"Green Thumb" originally published in *If*, April 1957. 1957.

"The Power and the Glory." Originally published as "The Man Who Would Not" in *If*, December 1969.

"The Listeners." Originally published in *Galaxy*, September 1968.

— *BL* JUL 2 '73

Contents

TRANSLATIONS

1. *Pues no es posible* . . .
   The bow cannot always stand bent, nor can human frailty subsist without some lawful recreation.

   Cervantes, *Don Quixote*

2. *Habe nun, ach! Philosophie,* . . .
   Now I have studied philosophy,
   Medicine and the law,
   And, unfortunately, theology,
   Wearily sweating, yet I stand now,
   Poor fool, no wiser than I was before;
   I am called Master, even Doctor,
   And for these last ten years have drawn
   My students, by the nose, up, down,
   Crosswise and crooked. Now I see
   That we can know nothing finally.

   Goethe, *Faust*, opening lines

3. *Men che dramma* . . .
   Less than a drop
   Of blood remains in me that does not tremble;
   I recognize the signals of the ancient flame.

   Dante, *The Divine Comedy*, Purgatorio

4. *C'est de quoy j'ay le plus de peur que la peur.*
   The thing of which I have most fear is fear.

   Montaigne, *Essays*

5. *A la très-bonne, à la très-belle, qui fait ma joie et ma santé.*
   To the best, to the most beautiful, who is my joy and my well-being.

   Baudelaire, *Les Epaves*

6. *Rast ich, so rost ich.*
When I rest, I rust.

German proverb

7. *Nunc est bibendum!*
Now's the time for drinking!

Horace, *Odes*, Book I

8. *Wer immer strebens sich bemüht,* . . .
Who strives always to the utmost,
Him can we save.

Goethe, *Faust*, Part I

9. *Ich bin der Geist der stets verneint.*
I am the spirit that always denies.

Goethe, *Faust*, Part I

10. *Nel mezzo del cammin di nostra vita* . . .
In the middle of the journey of our life
I came to myself in a dark wood,
Where the straight way was lost.

Dante, *The Divine Comedy*,
Inferno, opening lines

11. *E quindi uscimmo a riveder le stelle.*
And thence we issued out, again to see the stars.

Dante, *The Divine Comedy*,
Inferno

12. *Nil desperandum.*
There's no cause for despair.

Horace, *Odes*, Book I

13. *HIC • SITVS • EST • PHAETHON • CVRRVS •
AVRIGA •PATERNI* . . .
Here Phaeton lies: in Phoebus' car he fared,
And though he greatly failed, more greatly dared.

Ovid, *Metamorphoses*

14. *Percé jusques au fond du coeur* . . .
Pierced to the depth of my heart
By a blow unforseen and mortal.

Corneille, *Le Cid*

15. *Je m'en vay chercher un grand Peut-être.*
I am going to seek a great Perhaps.

Rabelais on his deathbed

16. *O lente, lente currite, noctis equi!*
Oh, slowly, slowly run, horses of the night!

Marlowe, *Dr. Faustus*

(Faustus is quoting Ovid. He waits for Mephis-
topheles to appear to claim his soul at midnight.
The next line: "The devil will come and Faustus
must be damn'd.")

17. *Meine Ruh' ist hin,* . . .
My peace is gone,
My heart is heavy.

Goethe, *Faust*, Part I

18. *Que acredito su ventura,* . . .
For if he like a madman lived,
At least he like a wise one died.

Cervantes, *Don Quixote*
(Don Quixote's epitaph)

19. *Ful wys is he that can himselven knowe!*
Very wise is he that can know himself!

Chaucer, *The Canterbury
Tales*, "The Monk's Tale"

20. *Pigmaei gigantum humeris impositi plusquam ipsi gigantes vidant.*
A dwarf standing on the shoulder of a giant may see further than the giant himself.

Didacus   Stella,   in
Lucan, *De Bello Civili*

Introduction

FOR NEARLY two hundred years—since the beginning of the Industrial Revolution in the mid-eighteenth century—science fiction was a part of the spectrum of general literature. It was so much a part of the rest of fiction that there wasn't even a name for it: the man who proved that science fiction could be popular, Jules Verne, called his novels "voyages extraordinaires"; the man who proved that science fiction could be art, H.G. Wells, found his earliest, most successful novels labeled "scientific romances."

Then in 1926 the German immigrant inventor, science enthusiast, and publishing entrepreneur, Hugo Gernsback, created the first science fiction magazine, *Amazing Stories*. He also invented a word to describe the kind of stories he was going to publish, "scientifiction"; it wasn't until 1929, when he had lost control of *Amazing Stories* and started a competing publication, *Wonder Stories*, that he created the phrase "science fiction." The creation of a science fiction magazine, then two, then a handful, affected science fiction like the invention of an impenetrable protective barrier; it created a golden ghetto in which science fiction could grow, buffered from contact with general literature and its critical demands, nourished by the enthusiasm and loyalty of its readers (only science fiction developed "fans," fan magazines, and conventions), and stimulated by the missionary spirit, the intellectual curiosity, and evolutionary development of its writers.

The first generation of science fiction writers learned their trade in the pulps; they wrote other kinds of category fiction —westerns, mysteries, war stories, sea stories, adventure stories—and they knew how to construct a plot full of action, suspense, and adventure, which would grab and hold a reader.

The second generation of science fiction writers were engineers and scientists; what they knew about characterization and plot they had learned from their predecessors, but their chief interest was the interrelationship between humanity and the universe, as it was and as it might be. The third generation of science fiction writers became concerned with sociological questions and the impact of technological change on the average individual.

Meanwhile, the mainstream seemed to be writing itself into a corner where its concern for technique left it nothing to write about except the nature of language. Gradually, almost independent of other literary influences, science fiction evolved through a process of self-criticism, self-development, and natural selection into the only field of fiction dealing seriously, either on a conscious or mythic level, with the issues of our times: change, the future, the machine, the city, pollution, overpopulation, space exploration, cataclysm, human survival, and all the rest of today's problems.

Eventually science fiction and general literature had to come together again, just as the detective story and the western, also brought to maturity in the pulp magazines, became acceptable general literary forms. Science fiction took a different route. The pulp magazines did not die like their brothers and sisters in other categories (indeed, they may have become the last refuge of the popular American short story). Mainstream writers began to adopt science fiction themes for their work: Barth, Boulle, Burroughs, Burgess, Golding, Hersey, Lessing, Nabakov, Rand, John Williams, Wouk, Vercors, Vonnegut, Voznesensky. . . . And the fourth generation of science fiction writers entered the field. They had grown up reading science fiction, but they also knew literature and the humanities and they wanted to write stories and novels which met the critical standards of the mainstream.

Writers of science fiction seem to be created in their youth when they encounter science fiction for the first time, are captured by its concepts, enraptured by its visions, stimulated by its intellectual conflicts. The new generation of writers, however, also are part of the alienated generation, and they have rejected much of the ethics and philosophy of the scientific culture in favor of the suspicions and anti-scientific viewpoint of the literary culture.

All of these generalizations are subject to many exceptions: adventure stories still form a significant part of science fiction, and hard science stories are written by younger writers. Similarly a concern for technique was exhibited by writers throughout the history of magazine science fiction, in the forties and fifties by writers like Ted Sturgeon, Alfred Bester, Ray Bradbury, James Blish, Damon Knight, William Tenn, Gordon Dickson, and others. Their approach was evolutionary; they tried to do better what science fiction has always done—tell a good story, dramatize possibilities, discuss alternatives, entertain with a conflict of ideas. When they were successful their stories helped to bridge the gap between science fiction and the mainstream, between the ghetto and the larger world outside, between C.P. Snow's two cultures.

The stories contained in this collection were intended as part of that effort. I called them then my "serious stories"; I look back upon them now as my attempts to bring to the task of telling a science fiction story everything I knew about setting and symbol, theme and character. Not all science fiction stories lend themselves to this approach; in many, the hero is society—or even an idea. These are stories about character—about beings in unusual circumstances facing difficult choices, pushed to the point where they must bend or break. Most of all, I hope they are stories that will involve and entertain. Interested readers may note the evolution of a writer.

The process of reunion continues, impelled by the pressure of the mainstream toward science fiction and the pressure of literarily oriented science fiction writers toward the mainstream. The future, even to the most farsighted science fiction writer, is obscure, but I have a feeling that both the mainstream and science fiction will be better for it, if, indeed, they are not once more one.

LAWRENCE, KANSAS

Nov. 8, 1971

1. *Breaking Point*

THEY SENT the advance unit out to scout the new planet in the *Ambassador,* homing down on the secret beeping of a featureless box dropped by an earlier survey party. Then they sat back at GHQ and began the same old pattern of worry that followed every advance unit.

Not about the ship. The *Ambassador* was a perfect machine: automatic, self-adjusting, self-regulating. It was built to last and do its job without failure, under any and all conditions, as long as there was a universe around it. And it could not fail. There was no question about that.

But an advance unit is composed of men. The factors of safety are indeterminable; the duplications of their internal mechanisms are conjectural, variable. The strength of the unit is the sum of the strengths of its members. The weakness of the unit can be a single small failing in a single man.

Beep . . . .boop . . .

"Gotcha!" said Ives. Ives was Communications. He had quick eyes, quick hands. He was huge, almost gross, but graceful. "On the nose," he grinned, and turned up the volume.

Beep . : . boop . . .

"What else do you expect?" said Johnny. Johnny was the Pilot—young, wide, flat. His movements were as controlled and decisive as those of the ship itself, in which he had an unshakeable faith. He slid into the bucket seat before the great master console.

Beep . . . boop . . .

"We expect the ship to do her job," said Hoskins, the Engineer. He was mild and deft, middle-aged, with a domed head and wide, light-blue eyes behind old-fashioned spectacles. He shared Johnny's belief in the machine, but through understanding rather than through admiration. "But it's always good to see her do it."

Beep . . . boop . . .

"Beautiful," said Captain Anderson softly, and he may have been talking about the way the ship was homing in on the tiny, featureless box that Survey had dropped on the unexplored planet, or about the planet itself, or even about the smooth integration of his crew.

Beep . . . boop . . .

Paresi said nothing. He had eyebrows and nostrils as sensitive as a radarscope, and masked eyes of a luminous black. Faces and motives were to him what gauges and log-entries were to the Engineer. Paresi was the Doctor, and he had many a salve and many a splint for invisible ills. He saw everything and understood much. He leaned against the bulkhead, his gaze flicking from one to the other of the crew. Occasionally his small mustache twitched like the antennae of a cat watching a bird.

Barely audible, faint as the blue outline of a distant hill, hungry and lost as the half-heard cry of a banshee, came the thin sound of high atmosphere against the ship's hull.

An hour passed.

Bup-bup-bup-bup . . .

"Shut that damned thing off!"

Ives looked up at the Pilot, startled. He turned the gain down to a whisper. Paresi left the bulkhead and stood behind Johnny. "What's the matter?" he asked. His voice was feline, too—a sort of purr.

Johnny looked up at him quickly, and grinned. "I can put her down," he said. "That's what I'm here for. I—like to think maybe I'll get to do it, that's all. I can't think that with the auto-pilot blasting out an 'on course'." He punched the veering-jet controls. It served men perfectly. The ship ignored him, homed on the beam. The ship computed velocity, altitude, gravity, magnetic polarization, windage; used and balanced and adjusted for them all. It adjusted for interference from the manual controls. It served men perfectly. It ignored them utterly.

Johnny turned to look out and downward. Paresi's gaze followed. It was a beautiful planet, perhaps a shade greener than the blue-green of earth. It seemed, indefinably, more park-like than wild. It had an air of controlled lushness and peace.

The braking-jets thundered as Johnny depressed a control. Paresi nodded slightly as he saw the Pilot's hand move, for he knew that the auto-pilot had done it, and that Johny's movement was one of trained reflex. The youngster was intense and alert, hair-trigger schooled, taught to pretend in such detail that the pretense was reality to him; a precise pretense that would become reality for all of them if the machine failed.

But, of course, the machine would not fail.

Fields fled beneath them, looking like a crazy-quilt in pastel. On them, nothing moved. Hoskins moved to the viewport and watched them mildly. "Very pastoral," he said. "Pretty."

"They haven't gotten very far," said Ives.

"Or they've gotten very far indeed," said Captain Anderson.

Johnny snorted. "No factories. No bridges. Cow-tracks and goat paths."

The Captain chuckled. "Some cultures go through an agrarian stage to reach a technological civilization, and some pass through technology to reach the pastoral."

"I don't see it," said Johnny shortly, eyes ahead.

Paresi's hand touched the Captain's arm, and the Captain then said nothing.

Pwing-g-g!

"Stand by for landing," said the Captain.

Ives and Hoskins went aft to the shock-panels in the after bulkhead. Paresi and the Captain stepped into niches flanking the console. Johnny touched a control that freed his chair in its hydraulic gimbals. Chair and niches and shock-panels would not be needed as long as the artificial gravity and inertialess field functioned; it was a ritual.

The ship skimmed treetops, heading phlegmatically for a rocky bluff. A gush of flame from its underjets and it shouldered heavily upward, just missing the jagged crest. A gout of fire forward, another, and it went into a long flat glide, following the fall of a foothill to the plain beyond. It held course and reduced speed, letting the ground billow up to it rather than descending. There was a moment of almost-flight, almost-sliding, and then a rush of dust and smoke which overtook and passed them. When it cleared, they were part of the plain, part of the planet.

"A good landing, John," Paresi said. Hoskins caught his eye and frowned. Paresi grinned broadly, and the exchange between them was clear: *Why do you needle the kid?* and *Quiet, Engine-room. I know what I'm doing.* Hoskins shrugged, and, with Ives, crossed to the communications desk.

Ives ran his fat, skilled hands over the controls and peered at his indicators. "It's more than a good landing," he grunted. "That squeak-box we homed in on can't be more than a hundred meters from here. First time I've ever seen a ship bull's-eye like that."

Johnny locked his gimbals, ran a steady, sensitive hand over the turn of the console as if it were a woman's flank. "Why—how close do you usually come?"

"Planetfall's close enough to satisfy Survey," said the Captain. "Once in a while the box will materialize conveniently on a continent. But this—this is too good to be true. We practically landed on it."

Hoskins nodded. "It's usually buried in some jungle, or at the bottom of a sea. But this is really all right. What a lineup! Point nine-eight earth gravity, Earth-type atmosphere—"

"Argon-rich," said Ives, from the panel. "Very rich."

"That'll make no real difference," Hoskins went on. "Temperature, about normal for an early summer back home . . . looks as if there's a fiendish plot afoot here to make things easy for us."

Paresi said, as if to himself, "I worry about easy things."

"Yeah, I know," snorted Johnny, rising to stretch. "The

head-shrinker always does it the hard way. You can't just dislike rice pudding; it has to be a sister-syndrome. If the shortest distance is from here to there, don't take it— remember your Uncle Oedipus."

Captain Anderson chuckled. "Cut your jets, Johnny. Maybe Paresi's tortuous reasoning does seem out of order on such a nice day. But remember—eternal vigilance isn't just the price of liberty, as the old books say. It's the price of existence. We know we're here—but we don't know where 'here' is, and won't until after we get back. This is *really* Terra Incognita. The location of Earth, or even of our part of the galaxy, is something that has to be concealed at all costs, until we're sure we're not going to turn up a potentially dangerous, possibly superior alien culture. What we don't know can't hurt Earth. No conceivable method could get that information out of us, any more than it could be had from the squeakbox that Survey dropped here.

"Base all your thinking on that, Johnny. If that seems like leaning over backward, it's only a sample of how careful we've got to be, how many angles we've got to figure."

"Hell," said the pilot. "I know all that. I was just ribbing the bat-snatcher here." He thumbed a cigarette out of his tunic, touched his lighter to it. He frowned, stared at the lighter, tried it again. "It doesn't work. *Damn* it!" he barked explosively. "I don't like things that don't work!"

Paresi was beside him, catlike, watchful. "Here's a light. Take it easy, Johnny! A bum lighter's not that important."

Johnny looked sullenly at his lighter. "It doesn't work," he muttered. "Guaranteed, too. When we get back I'm going to feed it to Supply." He made a vivid gesture to describe the feeding technique, and jammed the lighter back into his pocket.

"Heh!" Ives's heavy voice came from the communications desk. "Maybe the natives are primitives, at that. Not a whisper of any radio on any band. No powerline fields, either. These are plowboys, for sure."

Johnny looked out at the sleeping valley. His irritation over the lighter was still in his voice. "Imagine that. No video or trideo. No jet-races or feelies. What do people do with their time in a place like this?"

"Books," said Hoskins, almost absently. "Chess. Conversation."

"I don't know what chess is, and conversation's great if you want to tell somebody something, like 'bring me a steak'," said Johnny. "Let's get out of this firetrap," he said to the Captain.

"In time," said the Captain. "Ives, DX those radio frequencies. If there's so much as a smell of radiation even from the other side of this planet, we want to know about it. Hoskins, check the landing-suits—food, water, oxygen, radio, everything. Earth-type planet or no, we're not fooling with alien viruses. Johnny, I want you to survey this valley in every way you can and plot a minimum of three take-off vectors."

The crew fell to work, Ives and Hoskins intently, Johnny off-handedly, as if he were playing out a ritual with some children. Paresi bent over a stereomicroscope, manipulating controls which brought in samples of airborne bacteria and fungi and placed them under its objective. Captain Anderson ranged up beside him.

"We could walk out of the ship as if we were on Muroc Port," said Paresi. "These couldn't be more like Earth organisms if they'd been transplanted from home to delude us."

The Captain laughed. "Sometimes I tend to agree with Johnny. I never met a more suspicious character. How'd you ever bring yourself to sign your contract?"

"Turned my back on a couple of clauses," said Paresi. "Here—have a look."

At that moment the usually imperturbable Ives turned a sharp grunt that echoed and reechoed through the cabin. Paresi and the Captain turned. Hoskins was just coming out of the after alleyway with an oxygen bottle in his hand, and had frozen in his tracks at the sharp sound Ives had made. Johnny had whipped around as if the grunt had been a lion's roar. His back was to the bulkhead, his lean, long frame tensed for fight or flight. It was indescribable, Ives's grunt, and it was the only sound which could have had such an effect on such a variety of men—the same shocked immobility. Ives sat over his communications desk as if hypnotized by it. He moved one great arm forward, almost reluctantly, and turned a knob.

A soft, smooth hum filled the room. "Carrier," said Ives.

Then the words came. They were English words, faultlessly spoken, loud and clear and precise. They were harmless words, pleasant words even.

They were: "*Men of Earth! Welcome to our planet.*"

The voice hung in the air. The words stuck in the silence like insects wriggling upon a pin. Then the voice was gone, and the silence was complete and heavy. The carrier hum ceased. With a spine-tingling, brief blaze of high-frequency sound, Hoskins's oxygen bottle hit the steel deck.

Then they all began to breathe again.

"There's your farmers, Johnny," said Paresi.

"Knight to bishop's third," said Hoskins softly.

"What's that?" demanded Johnny.

"Chess again," said the Captain appreciatively. "An opening gambit."

Johnny put a cigarette to his lips, tried his lighter. "Damn. Gimme a light, Ives."

Ives complied, saying over his big shoulder to the Captain, "In case you wondered, there was no fix on that. My direction-finders indicate that the signal came simultaneously from forty-odd transmitters placed in a circle around the ship, which is their way of saying 'I dunno'."

The Captain walked to the view-bubble in front of the console and peered around. He saw the valley, the warm light of mid-afternoon, the too-green slopes, and the blue-green distances. Trees, rocks, a balancing bird.

"It doesn't work," muttered Johnny.

The Captain ignored him. " '*Men of Earth . . .*' " he quoted. "Ives, they've gotten into Survey's squeak-box and analyzed its origin. They know all about us!"

"They don't because they can't," said Ives flatly. "Survey traverses those boxes through second-order space. They materialize near a planet and drop in. No computation on earth or off it could trace their normal-space trajectory, let alone what happens in the second-order condition. The elements the box is made of are carefully averaged isotopic forms that could have come from any of nine galaxies we know about and probably more. And all it does is throw out a VUHF signal that says *beep* on one side, *boop* on the other, and *bup-bup* in between. It does *not* speak English, mention the planet Earth, announce anyone's arrival and purpose, or teach etiquette."

Captain Anderson spread his hands. "They got it from somewhere. They didn't get it from us. This ship and the box are the only Terran objects on this planet. Therefore they got their information from the box."

"Q.E.D. You reason like Euclid," said Paresi admiringly. "But don't forget that geometry is an artificial school, based on arbitrary axioms. It just doesn't work where the shortest distance is *not* a straight line . . . I'd suggest we gather evidence and postpone our conclusions."

"How do you think they got it?" Ives challenged.

"I think we can operate from the fact they got it, and make our analyses when we have more data."

Ives went back to his desk and threw a switch.

"What are you doing?" asked the Captain.

"Don't you think they ought to be answered?"

"Turn it off, Ives."

"But—"

"Turn it off!" Ives did. An expedition is an informal, highly democratic group, and can afford to be, for when the situation calls for it, there is never any question of where authority lies. The Captain said, "There is nothing we can say to them which won't yield them more information. Nothing. For all we know it may be very important to them to learn whether or not we received their message. Our countermove is obviously to make no move at all."

"You mean just sit here and wait until they do something else?" asked Johnny, appalled.

The Captain thumped his shoulder. "Don't worry. We'll do something in some other area than communications. Hoskins—are those landing-suits ready?"

"All but," rapped Hoskins. He scooped up the oxygen bottle and disappeared.

Paresi said, "We'll tell them something if we *don't* answer."

The Captain set his jaw. "We do what we can, Nick. We do the best we can. Got any better ideas?"

Paresi shrugged easily and smiled. "Just knocking, Skipper. Knock everything. Then what's hollow, you know about."

"I should know better than to jump salty with you," said the Captain, all but returning the Doctor's smile. "Johnny, Hoskins. Prepare for exploratory patrol."

"I'll go," said Paresi.

"Johnny goes," said the Captain bluntly, "because it's his first trip, and because if he isn't given something to do he'll bust his adrenals. Hoskins goes, because of all of us, the Engineer is most expendable. Ives stays because we need hair-trigger communications. I stay to correlate what goes on outside with what goes on inside. You stay because if anything goes wrong I'd rather have you fixing the men up than find myself trying to fix you up." He squinted at Paresi. "Does that knock solid?"

"Solid."

"Testing, Johnny," Ives said into a microphone. Johnny's duplicated voice, from the open face-plate of his helmet and from the intercom speaker, said, "I hear you fine."

"Testing, Hoskins."

"If I'd never seen you," said the speaker softly, "I'd think you were right here in the suit with me." Hoskins's helmet was obviously buttoned up.

The two men came shuffling into the cabin, looking like gleaming ghosts in their chameleon-suits, which repeated the color of the walls. "Someday," growled Johnny, "there'll be a type suit where you can scratch your—"

"Scratch when you get back," said the Captain. "Now hear this. Johnny, you can move fastest. You go out first. Wait in the airlock for thirty seconds after the outer port opens. When Ives gives you the beep, jump out, run around the bows, and plant your back against the hull directly opposite the port. Hold your blaster at the ready, aimed down—you hear me? *Down*, so that any observer will know you're armed, but not attacking. Hoskins, you'll be in the lock with the outer port open by that time. When Johnny gives the all clear, you'll jump out and put your back against the hull by the port. Then you'll both stay where you are until you get further orders. Is that clear?"

"Aye."

"Yup."

"You're covered adequately from the ship. Don't fire without orders. There's nothing you can get with a blaster that we can't get first with a projector—unless it happens to be within ten meters of the hull and we can't depress to it. Even then, describe it first and await orders to fire except in really extreme emergency. A single shot at the wrong time could set us back a thousand years with this planet. Remember that this ship isn't called *Killer* or *Warrior* or even *Hero*. It's the Earth Ship *Ambassador*. Go to it, and good luck."

Hoskins stepped back and waved Johnny past him. "After you, Jets."

Johnny's teeth flashed behind the face-plate. He clicked his heels and bowed stiffly from the waist, in a fine burlesque of an ancient courtier. He stalked past Hoskins and punched the button which controlled the airlock.

They waited. Nothing.

Johnny frowned, jabbed the button again. And again. The Captain started to speak, then fell watchfully silent. Johnny reached toward the button, touched it, then struck it savagely. He stepped back then, one foot striking the other like that of a clumsy child. He turned partially to the others. In his voice, as it came from the speaker across the room, was a deep amazement that rang like the opening chords of a prophetic and gloomy symphony.

He said, "The port won't open."

II

The extremes of mysticism and of pragmatism have their own expressions of worship. Each has its form, and the difference between them is the difference between deus ex machina *and* deus machina est.

—*E. Hunter Waldo*

"Of course it will open," said Hoskins. He strode past the

stunned Pilot and confidently palmed the control.

The port didn't open.

Hoskins said, "Hm?" as if he had been asked an inaudible question, and tried again. Nothing happened. "Skipper," he said over his shoulder, "have a quick look at the meters behind you there. Are we getting auxiliary power?"

"All well here," said Anderson after a glance at the board. "And no shorts showing."

There was a silence punctuated by the soft, useless clicking of the control as Hoskins manipulated it. "Well, what do you know."

"It won't work," said Johnny plaintively.

"Sure it'll work," said Paresi swiftly, confidently. "Take it easy, Johnny."

"It won't work," said Johnny. "It won't work." He stumbled across the cabin and leaned against the opposite bulkhead, staring at the closed port with his head a little to one side as if he expected it to shriek at him.

"Let me try," said Ives, going to Hoskins. He put out his hand.

"*Don't!*" Johnny cried.

"Shut up, Johnny," said Paresi.

"All right, Nick," said Johnny. He opened his face-plate, went to the rear bulkhead, keyed open an acceleration couch, and lay face down on it. Paresi watched him, his lips pursed.

"Can't say I blame him," said the Captain softly, catching Paresi's eye. "It's something of a shock. This shouldn't *be*. The safety factor's too great—a thousand percent or better."

"I know what you mean," said Hoskins. "I saw it myself, but I don't believe it." He pushed the button again.

"I believe it," said Paresi.

Ives went to his desk, clicked the transmitter and receiver switches on and off, moved a rheostat or two. He reached up to a wall-toggle, turned a small air-circulating fan on and off. "Everything else seems to work," he said absently.

"This is ridiculous!" exploded the Captain. "It's like leaving your keys home, or arriving at the theater without your tickets. It isn't dangerous—it's just stupid!"

"It's dangerous," said Paresi.

"Dangerous how?" Ives demanded.

"For one thing—" Paresi nodded toward Johnny, who lay tensely, his face hidden. "For another, the simple calculation that if nothing inside this ship made that control fail, something outside this ship did it. And *that* I don't like."

"That couldn't happen," said the Captain reasonably.

Paresi snorted impatiently. "Which of two mutually exclusive facts are you going to reason from? That the ship can't fail? Then this failure isn't a failure; it's an external control. Or are you going to reason that the ship *can* fail? Then you don't have to worry about an external force—but you can't trust anything about the ship. Do the trick that makes you happy. But do only one. You can't have both."

Johnny began to laugh.

Ives went to him. "Hey, boy—"

Johnny rolled over, swung his feet down, and sat up, brushing the fat man aside. "What you guys need," Johnny chuckled, "is a nice kind policeman to feed you candy and take you home. You're real lost."

Ives said, "Johnny, take it easy and be quiet, huh? We'll figure a way out of this."

"I already have, scrawny," said Johnny offensively. He got up, strode to the port. "What a bunch of deadheads," he growled. He went two steps past the port and grasped the control-wheel which was mounted on the other side of the port from the button.

"Oh my God," breathed Anderson delightedly, "the manual! Anybody else want to be Captain?"

"Factor of safety," said Hoskins, smiting himself on the brow. "There's a manual control for everything on this scow that there can be. And we stand here staring at it—"

"If we don't win the fur-lined teacup . . ." Ives laughed.

Johnny hauled on the wheel.

It wouldn't budge.

"Here—" Ives began to approach.

"Get away," said Johnny. He put his hands close together on the rim of the wheel, settled his big shoulders, and hauled. With a sharp crack the wheel broke off in his hands.

Johnny staggered, then stood. He looked at the wheel and

then up at the broken end of its shaft, gleaming deep below
the surface of the bulkhead.

"Oh, fine . . ." Ives whispered.

Suddenly Johnny threw back his head and loosed a burst
of high, hysterical laughter. It echoed back and forth between
the metal walls like a torrent from a burst dam. It went on
and on, as if now that the dam was gone, the flood would run
forever.

Anderson called out "Johnny!" three times, but the note of
command had no effect. Paresi walked to the Pilot and
slapped him sharply across the cheeks. "Johnny! Stop it!"

The laughter broke off as suddenly as it had begun.
Johnny's chest heaved, drawing in breath with great, rasping
near-sobs. Slowly they died away. He extended the wheel
toward the Captain.

"It broke off," he said finally, dully, without emphasis.

Then he leaned back against the hull, slowly slid down
until he was sitting on the deck. "Broke right off," he said.

Ives twined his fat fingers together and bent them until the
knuckles cracked. "Now what?"

"I suggest," said Paresi, in an extremely controlled tone,
"that we all sit down and think over the whole thing very
carefully."

Hoskins had been staring hypnotically at the broken shaft
deep in the wall. "I wonder," he said at length, "which way
Johnny turned that wheel."

"Counter-clockwise," said Ives. "You saw him."

"I know that," said Hoskins. "I mean, which way: the right
way, or the wrong way?"

"Oh." There was a short silence. Then Ives said, "I guess
we'll never know now."

"Not until we get back to Earth," said Paresi quickly.

"You say 'until,' or 'unless'?" Ives demanded.

"I said 'until,' Ives," said Paresi levelly, "and watch your
mouth."

"Sometimes," said the fat man with a dangerous joviality,
"you pick the wrong way to say the right thing, Nick." Then
he clapped the slender Doctor on the back. "But I'll be good.
We sow no panic seed, do we?"

"Much better not to," said the Captain. "It's being done efficiently enough from outside."

"You are convinced it's being done from outside?" asked Hoskins, peering at him owlishly.

"I'm . . . convinced of very little," said the Captain heavily. He went to the acceleration couch and sat down. "I want out," he said. He waved away the professional comment he could see forming on Paresi's lips and went on, "Not claustrophobia, Nick. Getting out of the ship's more important than just relieving our feelings. If the trouble with the port is being caused by some fantastic *something* outside this ship, we'll achieve a powerful victory over it, purely by ignoring it."

"It broke off," murmured Johnny.

"Ignore *that*," snorted Ives.

"You keep talking about this thing being caused by something outside," said Paresi. His tone was almost complaining.

"Got a better hypothesis?" asked Hoskins.

"Hoskins," said the Captain, "isn't there some way we can get out? What about the tubes?"

"Take a shipyard to move those power-plants," said Hoskins, "and even if it could be done, those radioactive tubes would fry you before you crawled a third of the way."

"We should have a lifeboat," said Ives to no one in particular.

"What in time does a ship like the *Ambassador* need with a lifeboat?" asked Hoskins in genuine amazement.

The Captain frowned. "What about the ventilators?"

"Take us days to remove all the screens and purifiers," said Hoskins, "and then we'd be up against the intake ports. You could stroll out through any of them about as far as your forearm. And after that it's hull-metal, Skipper. *That* you don't cut, not with a piece of the Sun's core."

The Captain got up and began pacing, slowly and steadily, as if the problem could be trodden out like ripe grapes. He closed his eyes and said, "I've been circling around that idea for thirty minutes now. Look: the hull can't be cut because it is built so it can't fail. It doesn't fail. The port controls were also built so they wouldn't fail. They do fail. The thing that keeps us in stays in shape. The thing that lets us out goes bad. Effect: we stay inside. Cause: something that wants us to stay inside."

"Oh," said Johnny clearly.

They looked at him. He raised his head, stiffened his spine against the bulkhead. Paresi smiled at him. "Sure, Johnny. The machine didn't fail. It was—controlled. It's all right." Then he turned to the Captain and said carefully, "I'm not denying what you say, Skipper. But I don't like to think of what will happen if you take that tack, reason it through, and don't get any answers."

"I'd hate to be a psychologist," said Ives fervently. "Do you extrapolate your mastications, too, and get frightened of the stink you might get?"

Paresi smiled coldly. "I control my projections."

Captain Anderson's lips twitched in passing amusement, and then his expression sobered. "I'll take the challenge, Paresi. We have a cause and an effect. Something is keeping us in the ship. Corollary: We—or perhaps the ship—we're not welcome."

"*Men of Earth*," quoted Ives, in an excellent imitation of the accentless English they had heard on the radio, "*welcome to our planet.*"

"They're kidding," said Johnny heartily, rising to his feet. He dropped the control wheel with a clang and shoved it carelessly aside with his foot. "Who ever says exactly what they mean anyhow? I see that conclusion the head-shrinker's afraid you'll get to, Skipper. If we can't leave the ship, the only other thing we can do is to leave the planet. That it?"

Paresi nodded and watched the Captain closely. Anderson turned abruptly away from them all and stood, feet apart, head down, hands behind his back, and stared out of the forward viewports. In the tense silence they could hear his knuckles crack. At length he said quietly, "That isn't what we came here for, Johnny."

Johnny shrugged. "Okay. Chew it up all you like, fellers. The only other choice is to sit here like bugs in a bottle until we die of old age. When you get tired of thinking that over, just let me know. I'll fly you out."

"We can always depend on Johnny," said Paresi with no detectable emphasis at all.

"Not on me," said Johnny, and swatted the bulkhead. "On the ship. Nothing on any planet can stop this baby once I pour on the coal. She's just got too much muscle."

"Well, Captain?" asked Hoskins softly.

Anderson looked at the basking valley, at the too-blue sky, and the near-familiar, mellow-weathered crags. They waited.

"Take her up," said the Captain. "Put her in orbit at two hundred kilos. I'm not giving up this easily."

Ives swatted Johnny's broad shoulder. "That's a take-off *and* a landing, if I know the Old Man. Go to it, Jets."

Johnny's wide white grin flashed and he strode to the control chair. "Gentlemen, be seated."

"I'll take mine lying down," said Ives, and spread his bulk out on the acceleration couch. The others went to their take-off posts.

"On automatics," said the Captain, "Fire away!"

"Fire away!" said Johnny cheerfully. He reached forward and pressed the central control.

Nothing happened

Johnny put his hand toward the control again. It moved as if there were a repellor field around the button. The hand moved more and more slowly the closer it got, until it hovered just over the control and began to tremble.

"On manual," barked the Captain. "Fire!"

"Manual, sir," said Johnny reflexively. His trembling hand darted up to an overhead switch, pulled it. He grasped the control bars and dropped the heels of his hands heavily on the firing studs. From somewhere came a muted roar, a whispering; a subjective suggestion of the thunder of reaction motors.

A frown crossed Paresi's face. The rocket noise was gone as the mind reached for it, like an occluded thought. The motors were silent; there wasn't a tremor of vibration. Yet somewhere a ghost engine was warming up, preparing a ghost ship for an intangible take-off into nothingness.

He snapped off the catch of his safety belt and crossed

swiftly and silently to the console. Johnny sat raptly. A slow smile of satisfaction began to spread over his face. His gaze flicked to dials and gauges; he nodded very slightly, and brought both hands down like an organist playing a mighty chord. He watched the gauges. The needles were still, lying on their zero pins, and, where lights should have flickered and flashed, there was nothing. Paresi glanced at Anderson and met a worried look. Hoskins had his head cocked to one side, listening, puzzled. Ives rose from the couch and came forward to stand beside Paresi.

Johnny was manipulating the keys firmly. His fingers began to play a rapid, skillful, silent concerto. His face had a look of intense concentration and of complete self-confidence.

"Well," said Ives heavily. "That's a bust, too."

Paresi spun to him. "*Shh!*" It was done with such intensity that Ives recoiled. With a warning look at him, Paresi walked to the Captain, whispered in his ear.

"My God," said Anderson. "All right, Doctor." He came forward to the Pilot's chair. Johnny was still concentratedly, uselessly at work. Anderson glanced inquiringly at Paresi, who nodded.

"That does it," said the Captain, loudly. "Nice work, Johnny. We're smack in orbit. The automatics couldn't have done it better. For once it feels good to be out in space again. Cut your jets now. You can check for correction later."

"Aye, sir," said Johnny. He made two delicate adjustments, threw a master switch and swung around. "Whew! That's work!"

Facing the four silent men, Johnny thumbed out a cigarette, put it in his mouth, touched his lighter to it, drew a long slow puff.

"Man, that goes good . . ."

The cigarette was not lighted. Hoskins turned away, an expression of sick pity on his face. Ives reached abruptly for his own lighter, and the Doctor checked him with a gesture.

"Every time I see a hot pilot work I'm amazed," Paresi said conversationally. "Such concentration . . . you must be tuckered, Johnny."

Johnny puffed at his unlit cigarette. "Tuckered," he said. "Yeah." There were two odd undertones to his voice suddenly. They were fatigue and eagerness. Paresi said, "You're off-watch, John. Go stretch out."

"Real tired," mumbled Johnny. He lumbered to his feet and went aft, where he rolled to the couch and was asleep almost instantly.

The others congregated far forward around the controls, and for a long moment stared silently at the sleeping Pilot.

"I don't get it," murmured Ives.

"He really thought he flew us out, didn't he?" asked Hoskins.

Paresi nodded. "Had to. There isn't any place in his cosmos for machines that don't work. Contrary evidence can get just so strong. Then, for him, it ceased to exist. A faulty cigarette lighter irritated him, a failing airlock control made him angry and sullen and then hysterical. When the drive controls wouldn't respond, he reached his breaking point. Everyone has such a breaking point, and arrives at it just that way if he's pushed far enough."

"Everyone?"

Paresi looked from face to face, and nodded somberly. Anderson asked, "What knocked him out? He's trained to take far more strain than that."

"Oh, he isn't suffering from any physical or conscious mental fatigue. The one thing he wanted to do was to get away from a terrifying situation. He convinced himself that he flew out of it. The next best thing he could do to keep anything else from attacking him was to sleep. He very much appreciated my suggestion that he was worn out and needed to stretch out."

"I'd very much appreciate some such," said Ives. "Do it to me, Nick."

"Reach your breaking point first," said the Doctor flatly, and went to place a pillow between Johnny's head and a guard-rail.

Hoskins turned away to stare at the peaceful landscape outside. The Captain watched him for a moment, then: "Hoskins!"

"Aye."

"I've seen that expression before. What are you thinking about?"

The Engineer looked at him, shrugged, and said mildly, "Chess."

"What, especially?"

"Oh, a very general thing. The reciprocity of the game. That's what makes it the magnificent thing it is. Most human enterprises can gang up on a man, slap him with one disaster after another without pause. But not chess. No matter who your opponent might be, every time he does something to you, *it's your move.*"

"Very comforting. Have you any idea of how we move now?"

Hoskins looked at him, a gentle surprise on his aging face. "You missed my point. Skipper. *We* don't move."

"Oh," the Captain whispered. His face tautened as it paled. "I . . . I see. We pushed the airlocks button to get out. Countermove: It wouldn't work. We tried the manual. Countermove: It broke off. And so on. Now we've tried to fly the ship out. Oh, but Hoskins—Johnny broke. Isn't that countermove enough?"

"Maybe. Maybe you're right. Maybe the move wasn't trying the drive controls, though. Maybe the move was to do what was necessary to knock Johnny out." He shrugged again. "We'll very soon see."

The Captain exhaled explosively through his nostrils. "We'll find out if it's our move by moving," he gritted. "Ives! Paresi! We're going to go over this thing from the beginning. First, try the port. You, Ives."

Ives grunted and went to the ship's side. Then he stopped. "Where is the port?"

Anderson and Paresi followed Ives's flaccid, shocked gaze to the bulkhead where there had been the outline of the closed port, and beside it the hole which had held the axle of the manual wheel, and which now was a smooth, seamless curtain of impenetrable black. But Hoskins looked at the Captain first of all, and he said "*Now* it's our move," and only then did he turn with them to look at the darkness.

III

The unfamiliar, you say, is the unseen, the completely new and strange? Not so. The epitome of the unfamiliar is the familiar inverted, the familiar turned on its head. View a familiar place under new conditions—a deserted and darkened theater, an empty nightclub by day—and you will find yourself more influenced by the emotion of strangeness than by any number of unseen places. Go back to your old neighborhood and find everything changed. Come into your own home when everyone is gone, when the lights are out and the furniture rearranged—there I will show you the strange and frightening ghosts that are the shapes left over when reality superimposes itself upon the images of memory. The goblins lurk in the shadows of your own room . . .

—*Owen Miller*
ESSAYS ON NIGHT AND THE UNFAMILIAR

For one heart-stopping moment the darkness had seemed to swoop in upon them like the clutching hand of death. Instinctively they had huddled together in the center of the room. But when the second look, and the third, gave them reassurance that the effect was really there, though the cause was still a mystery, then half the mystery was gone, and they began to drift apart. Each felt on trial, and held tight to himself and the picture of himself he emphasized in the others' eyes.

The Captain said quietly, "It's just . . . there. It doesn't seem to be spreading."

Hoskins gazed at it critically. "About half-a-meter deep," he murmured. "What do you suppose it's made of?"

"Not a gas," said Paresi. "It has a—a sort of surface."

Ives, who had frozen to the spot when first he saw the blackness on his way to the port, took another two steps. The hand, which had been half-lifted to touch the control, continued upward relievedly, as if glad to have a continuous function even though its purpose had changed.

"Don't touch it!" rapped the Captain.

Ives turned his head to look at the Captain, then faltered and let the hand drop. "Why not?"

"Certainly not a liquid," Paresi mused, as if there had been no interruption. "And if it's a solid, where did that much matter come from? Through the hull?"

Hoskins, who knew the hull, how it was made, how fitted, how treated once it was in place, snorted at the idea.

"If it was a gas," said Paresi, "there'd be diffusion. *And* convection. If it were poisonous, we'd all be dead. If not, the chances are we'd smell it. And the counter's not saying a thing—so it's not radioactive."

"You trust the counter?" asked Ives bitterly.

"I trust it," said Paresi. His near-whisper shook with what sounded like passion. "A man must have faith in something. I hold that faith in every single function of every part of this ship until each and every part is separately and distinctly proved unworthy of faith!"

"Then, by God, you'll understand my faith in my own two hands and what they feel," snarled Ives. He stepped to the bulkhead and brought his meaty hand hard against it.

"*Touché*," murmured Hoskins, and meant either Ives's remark or the flat, solid smack of the hand against the blackness.

In his sleep, Johnny uttered a high, soft, careless tinkle of youthful, happy laughter.

"Somebody's happy," said Ives.

"Paresi," said the Captain, "what happens when he wakes up?"

Paresi's eyebrows shrugged for him. "Practically anything. He's reached down inside himself, somewhere, and found a way out. For him—not for any of the rest of us. Maybe he'll ignore what we see. Maybe he'll think he's somewhere else, or in some other time. Maybe he'll *be* someone else. Maybe he won't wake up at all."

"Maybe he has the right idea," said Ives.

"That's the second time you've made a crack like that," said Paresi levelly. "Don't do it again. You can't afford it."

"*We* can't afford it," the Captain put in.

"All right," said Ives, with such docility that Paresi shot him a startled, suspicious glance. The big Communications man went to his station and sat, half-turned away from the rest.

"What are they after?" complained the Captain suddenly. "What do they want?"

"Who?" asked Paresi, still watching Ives.

Hoskins explained, "Whoever it was who said, '*Welcome to our planet.*' "

Ives turned toward them, and Paresi's relief was noticeable. Ives said, "They want us dead."

"Do they?" asked the Captain.

"They don't want us to leave the ship, and they don't want the ship to leave the planet."

"Then it's the ship they want."

"Yeah," amended Ives, "without us."

Paresi said, "You can't conclude that, Ives. They've inconvenienced us. They've turned us in on ourselves, and put a drain on our intangible resources as men and as a crew. But so far they haven't actually done anything to us. We've done it to ourselves."

Ives looked at him scornfully. "We wrecked the unwreckable controls, manufactured that case-hardened darkness, and talked to ourselves on an all-wave carrier with no source, about information no outsider could get?"

"I didn't say any of that." Paresi paused to choose words. "Of course they're responsible for these phenomena. But the phenomena haven't hurt us. Our reactions to the phenomena are what have done the damage."

"A fall never hurt anyone, they told me when I was a kid," said Ives pugnaciously. "It's the sudden stop."

Paresi dismissed the remark with a shrug. "I still say that while we have been astonished, frightened, puzzled, and frustrated, we have not been seriously threatened. Our water and food and air are virtually unlimited. Our ability to live with one another under emergency situations has been tested to a fare-thee-well, and all we have to do is recognize the emergency as such and that ability will rise to optimum." He smiled suddenly. "It could be worse, Ives."

"I suppose it could," said Ives. "That blackness could move in until it really crowded us, or—"

Very quietly Hoskins said, "It *is* moving in."

Captain Anderson shook his head. "No . . ." And hearing him, they slowly recognized that the syllable was not a denial, but an exclamation. For the darkness was no longer a half-meter deep on the bulkhead. No one had noticed it, but they suddenly became aware that the almost-square cabin was now definitely rectangular, with the familiar controls, the communications wall, and the thwartship partition aft of them forming three sides to the encroaching fourth.

Ives rose shaking and round-eyed from his chair. He made an unspellable animal sound and rushed at the blackness. Paresi leaped for him, but not fast enough. Ives collided sickeningly against the strange jet surface and fell. He fell massively, gracelessly, not prone but on wide-spread knees, with his arms crumpled beneath him and the side of his face on the deck. He stayed there, quite unconscious, a gross caricature of worship.

There was a furiously active, silent moment while Paresi turned the fat man over on his back, ran skilled fingers over his bleeding face, his chest, back to the carotid area of his neck. "He's all right," said Paresi, still working; then, as if to keep his mind going with words to avoid conjecture, he went on didactically. "This is the other fear reaction. Johnny's was 'flight,' Ives's is 'fight.' The empirical result is very much the same."

"I thought," said Hoskins dryly, "that fight and flight were survival reactions."

Paresi stood up. "Why, they are. In the last analysis, so is suicide."

"I'll think about that," said Hoskins softly.

"Paresi!" spat Anderson. "Medic or no, you'll watch your mouth!"

"Sorry, Captain. That was panic seed. Hoskins—"

"Don't explain it to me," said the Engineer mildly. "I know what you meant. Suicide's the direct product of survival compulsions—drives that try to save something, just as fight and flight are efforts to save something. I don't think you

need worry; immolation doesn't tempt me. I'm too—too interested in what goes on. What are you going to do about
Ives?"

"Bunk him, I guess, and stand by to fix up that headache
he'll wake up to. Give me a hand, will you?"

Hoskins went to the bulkhead and dropped a second acceleration couch. It took all three of them, working hard, to lift
Ives's great bulk up to it. Paresi opened the first-aid kit
clamped under the control console and went to the unconscious man. The Captain cast about him for something to do,
something to say, and apparently found it. "Hoskins!"

"Aye."

"Do you usually think better on an empty stomach?"

"Not me."

"I never have either."

Hoskins smiled. "I can take a hint. I'll rassle up something
hot and filling."

"Good man," said the Captain, as Hoskins disappeared
toward the after quarters. Anderson walked over to the Doctor and stood watching him clean up the abraded bruise on
Ives's forehead.

Paresi, without looking up, said, "You'd better say it, whatever it is. Get it out."

Anderson half-chuckled. "You psychic?"

Paresi shot him a glance. "Depends. If you mean has a natural sensitivity to the tension spectra coupled itself with
some years of practice in observing people—then yes.
What's on your mind?"

Anderson said nothing for a long time. It was as if he were
waiting for a question, a single prod from Paresi. But Paresi
wouldn't give it. Paresi waited, just waited, with his dark face
turned away, not helping, not pushing, not doing a single
thing to modify the pressure that churned about in the Captain.

"All right," said the Captain irritably. "I'll tell you."

Paresi took tweezers, a retractor, two scalpels, and a hypo-
dermic case out of the kit and laid them in a neat row on the
bunk. He then picked up each one and returned it to the kit.
When he had quite finished Anderson said, "I was wonder-

ing, *who's next?*"

Paresi nodded and shut the kit with a sharp click. He looked up at the Captain and nodded again. "Why does it have to be you?" he asked.

"I didn't say it would be me!" said the Captain sharply.

"Didn't you?" When the Captain had no answer, Paresi asked him, "Then why wonder about a thing like that?"

"Oh . . . I see what you mean. When you start to be afraid, you start to be unsure—not of anyone else's weaknesses, but of your own. That what you mean?"

"Yup." His dark-framed grin flashed suddenly. "But you're not afraid, Cap'n."

"The hell I'm not."

Paresi shook his head. "Johnny was afraid, and fled. Ives was afraid, and fought. There's only one fear that's a real fear, and that's the one that brings you to your breaking point. Any other fear is small potatoes compared with a terror like that. Small enough so no one but me has to worry about it."

"Why you, then?"

Paresi swatted the first-aid kit as he carried it back to its clamp. "I'm the M.O. remember? Symptoms are my business. Let me watch 'em, Captain. Give me orders, but don't crowd me in my specialty."

"You're insubordinate, Paresi," said Anderson, "and you're a great comfort." His slight smile faded, and horizontal furrows appeared over his eyes. "Tell me why I had that nasty little phase of doubt about myself."

"You think I can?"

"Yes." He was certain.

"That's half the reason. The other half is Hoskins."

"What are you talking about?"

"Johnny broke. Ives broke. Your question was, 'Who's next?' You doubt that it will be me, because I'm *de facto* the boy with all the answers. You doubt it will be Hoskins, because you can't extrapolate how he might break—or even if he would. So that leaves you."

"I hadn't exactly reasoned it out like that—"

"Oh yes you had," said Paresi, and thumped the Captain's shoulder. "Now forget it. Confucius say he who turn gaze inward wind up cross-eyed. Can't afford to have a cross-eyed Captain. Our friends out there are due to make another move."

"No they're not."

The Doctor and the Captain whirled at the quiet voice. "What does *that* mean, Hoskins?"

The Engineer came into the cabin, crossed over to his station, and began opening and closing drawers. "They've moved." From the bottom drawer he pulled out a folded chessboard and a rectangular box. Only then did he look directly at them. "The food's gone."

"Food?. . . gone where?"

Hoskins smiled tiredly. "Where's the port? Where's the outboard bulkhead? That black stuff has covered it up—heading units, foodlockers, disposal unit, everything." He pulled a couple of chairs from their clips on the bulkhead and carried them across the cabin to the sheet of blackness. "There's water," he said as he unfolded the chairs. On the seat of one he placed the chessboard. He sat on the other and pushed the board close to the darkness. "The scuttlebutt's inboard, and still available." His voice seemed to get fainter and fainter as he talked, as if he were going slowly away from them. "But there's no food. No food."

He began to set up the pieces, his face to the black wall.

IV

The primary function of personality is self-preservation, but personality itself is not a static but a dynamic thing. The basic factor in its development is integration; each new situation calls forth a new adjustment which modifies or alters the personality in the process. The proper aim of personality, therefore, is not permanence and stability, but unification. The inability of a personality to adjust to or integrate a new situation, the resistance of the personality to unification, and its efforts to preserve its integrity are known popularly as insanity.

—Morgan Littlefield,
NOTES ON PSYCHOLOGY.

"*Hoskins!*"

Paresi grabbed the Captain's arm and spun him around roughly. "Captain Anderson! Cut it!" Very softly, he said, "Leave him alone. He's doing what he has to do."

Anderson stared over his shoulder at the little Engineer. "Is he, now? Damn it, he's still under orders!"

"Got something for him to do?" asked the Doctor cooly.

Anderson looked around, at the controls, out at the sleeping mountains. "I guess not. But I'd like to know he'd take an order when I have one."

"Leave him alone until you have an order. Hoskins is a very steady head, Skipper. But just now he's on the outside edge. Don't push."

The Captain put his hand over his eyes and fumbled his way to the controls. He turned his back to the Pilot's chair and leaned heavily against it. "Okay," he said. "This thing is developing into a duel between you and those . . . those colleagues of yours out there. I guess the least we . . . I . . . can do is not to fight you while you're fighting them."

Paresi said, "You're choosing up sides the wrong way. They're fighting us, all right. We're only fighting ourselves. I don't mean each other; I mean each of us is fighting himself. We've got to stop doing that, Skipper."

The Captain gave him a wan smile. "Who has, at the best of times?"

Paresi returned the smile. "Drug addicts . . . catatonics . . . illusionaries . . . and saints. I guess it's up to us to add to the category."

"How about dead people?"

"Ives! How long have you been awake?"

The big man shoved himself up and leaned on one arm. He shook his head and grunted as if he had been punched in the solar plexus. "Who hit me with what?" he said painfully, from between clenched teeth.

"You apparently decided the bulkhead was a paper hoop and tried to dive through it," said Paresi. He spoke lightly but his face was watchful.

"Oooh . . ." Ives held his head for a moment and then peered between his fingers at the darkness. "I remember," he

said in a strained whisper. He looked around him, saw the
Engineer huddled against his chessboard. "What's he
doing?"

They all looked at the Engineer as he moved a piece and
then sat quietly.

"Hey, Hoskins!"

Hoskins ignored Ives's bull-voice. Paresi said, "He's not
talking just now. He's . . . all right, Ives. Leave him alone.
At the moment, I'm more interested in you. How do you
feel?"

"Me? I feel great. Hungry, though. What's for chow?"

Anderson said quickly, "Nick doesn't want us to eat just
now."

"Thanks," muttered Paresi in vicious irony.

"He's the Doctor," said Ives good-naturedly. "But don't
put it off too long, huh? This furnace needs stoking." He fist-
ed his huge chest.

"Well, this is encouraging," said Paresi.

"It certainly is," said the Captain. "Maybe the breaking
point is just the point of impact. After that the rebound, hm?"

Paresi shook his head. "Breaking means breaking. Sometimes things just don't break."

"Got to pass," said a voice. Johnny, the Pilot, was stirring.

"Ha!" Anderson's voice was exultant. "Here comes another one!"

"How sure are you of that?" asked the Doctor. To Johnny,
he called, "Hiya, John."

"I got to pass," said Johnny worriedly. He swung his feet
to the deck. "You see," he said earnestly, "being the head of
your class doesn't make it any easier. You've got to keep that
and pass the examinations too. You've got two jobs. Now, the
guy who stands fourth, say—he has only one job to do."

Anderson turned a blank face to Paresi, who made a silenc-
ing gesture. Johnny put his head in his hands and said,
"When one variable varies directly as another, two pairs of
their corresponding values are in proportion." He looked
up. "That's supposed to be the keystone of all vector analysis, the man says, and you don't get to be a pilot with-

out vector analysis. And it makes no sense to me. What am I going to do?"

"Get some shut-eye," said Paresi immediately. "You've been studying too hard. It'll make more sense to you in the morning."

Johnny grinned and yawned at the same time, the worried wrinkles smoothing out. "Now that was a real educational remark, Martin, old chap," he said. He lay down and stretched luxuriously. "*That* I can understand. You may wear my famous maroon zipsuit." He turned his face away and was instantly asleep.

"Who the hell is Martin?" Ives demanded. "Martin who?"

"Shh. Probably his roommate in pre-pilot school."

Anderson gaped. "You mean he's back in school?"

"Doesn't it figure?" said Paresi sadly. "I told you that this situation is intolerable to him. If he can't escape in space, he'll escape in time. He hasn't the imagination to go forward, so he goes backward."

Something scuttled across the floor. Ives whipped his feet off the floor and sat like some cartoon of a Buddha, clutching his ankles. "What in God's name was that?"

"I didn't see anything," said Paresi.

The Captain demanded, "What was it?"

From the shadows, Hoskins said, "A mouse."

"Nonsense."

"I can't stand things that scuttle and slither and crawl," said Ives. His voice was suddenly womanish. "Don't let anything like that in here!"

From the quarters aft came a faint scratching, a squeak. Ives turned pale. His wattles quivered.

"Snap out of it, Ives," said Paresi coldly. "There isn't so much as a microbe on this ship that I haven't inventoried. Don't sit there like little Miss Muffet."

"I know what I saw," said Ives. He rose suddenly, turned to the black wall, and bellowed, "Damn you, send something I can fight!"

Two mice emerged from under the couch. One of them ran over Ives's foot. They disappeared aft, squeaking. Ives leapt straight up and came down standing on the couch. Anderson stepped back against the inboard bulkhead and stood rigid. Paresi walked with great purpose to the medical chest, took out a small black case and opened it.

Ives cowered down to his knees and began to blubber openly, without attempting to hide it, without any articulate speech. Paresi approached him, half-concealing a small metal tube in his hand.

A slight movement on the deck caught Anderson's eye. He was unable to control a shrill intake of breath as an enormous spider, hairy and swift, darted across to the couch and sprang. It landed next to Ives's knee, sprang again. Paresi swung at it and missed, his hand catching Ives heavily just under the armpit. The spider hit the deck, skidded, righted itself and, abruptly, was gone. Ives caved in around the impact point of Paresi's hand and curled up silently on the couch. Anderson ran to him.

"He'll be all right now," said Paresi. "Forget it."

"Don't tell me he fainted! Not Ives!"

"Of course not." Paresi held up the little cylinder.

"Anesthox! Why did you use that on him?"

Paresi said irritably, "For the reason one usually uses anesthox. To knock a patient out for a couple of hours without hurting him."

"Suppose you hadn't?"

"How much more of that scuttle-and-slither treatment do you think he could have taken?"

Anderson looked at the unconscious Communications man. "Surely more than that." He looked up suddenly. "Where the hell *did* that vermin come from?"

"Ah. Now you have it. He dislikes mice and spiders. But there was something special about these. They couldn't be here, and they were. He felt that it was a deliberate and personal attack. He couldn't have handled much more of it."

"Where did they come from?" demanded the Captain again.

"*I* don't know!" snapped Paresi. "Sorry, Skipper . . . I'm a little unnerved. I'm not used to seeing a patient's hallucinations. Not that clearly, at any rate."

"They were Ives's hallucinations?"

"Can you recall what was said just before they appeared?"

"Uh . . . something scuttled. A mouse."

"It wasn't a mouse until someone said it was." The Doctor turned and looked searchingly at Hoskins, who still sat quietly over his chess.

"By God, it was Hoskins. Hoskins—what made you say that?"

The Engineer did not move nor answer. Paresi shook his head hopelessly. "Another retreat. It's no use, Captain."

Anderson took a single step toward Hoskins, then obviously changed his mind. He shrugged and said, "All right. Something scuttled and Hoskins defined it. Let's accept that without reasoning it out. So who called up the spider?"

"You did."

"*I* did?"

In a startling imitation of the Captain's voice, Paresi quoted, "Don't sit there like Miss Muffet!"

"I'll be damned," said Anderson. "Maybe we'd all be better off saying nothing."

Paresi said bitterly, "You think it makes any difference if we *say* what we think?"

"Perhaps . . ."

"Nope," said Paresi positively. "Look at the way this thing works. First it traps us, and then it shows us a growing darkness. Very basic. Then it starts picking on us, one by one. Johnny gets machines that don't work, when with his whole soul he worships machines that do. Ives gets a large charge of claustrophobia from the black stuff over there and goes into a flat spin."

"He came out of it."

"Johnny woke up too. In another subjective time-track. Quite harmless to—to Them. So they left him alone. But they lowered the boom on Ives when he showed any resilience. It's breaking point they're after, Captain. Nothing less."

"Hoskins?"

"I guess so," said Paresi tiredly. "Like Johnny he escaped from a problem he couldn't handle to one he could. Only instead of regressing he's turned to chess. I hope Johnny doesn't bounce back for awhile, yet. He's too—Captain! He's gone!"

They turned and stared at Johnny's bunk. Or—where the bunk had been before the black wall had swelled inwards and covered it.

V

"... and there I was, Doctor, in the lobby of the hotel at noon, stark naked!"

"Do you have these dreams often?"

"I'm afraid so, Doctor. Am I—all right? I mean . . ."

"Let me ask you this question: Do you believe that these experiences are real?"

"Of course not!"

"Then, Madam, you are, by definition, sane; for insanity, in the final analysis, is the inability to distinguish the real from the unreal."

Paresi and the Captain ran aft together, and together they stopped four paces away from the bulging blackness.

"Johnny!" The Captain's voice cracked with the agonized effort of his cry. He stepped to the black wall, pounded it with the heel of his hand.

"He won't hear you," said Paresi bleakly. "Come back, Captain. Come back."

"Why him? Why Johnny? They've done everything they could to Johnny; you said so yourself!"

"Come back," Paresi said again, soothing. Then he spoke briskly: "Can't you see they're not doing anything to him? They're doing it to us!"

The Captain stood rigidly, staring at the featureless intrusion. He turned presently. "To us," he parroted. Then he stumbled blindly to the Doctor, who put a firm hand on his biceps and walked with him to the forward acceleration couch.

The Captain sat down heavily with his back to this new invasion. Paresi stood by him reflectively, then walked silently to Hoskins.

The Engineer sat over his chessboard in deep concentration. The far edge of the board seemed to be indefinite, lost partially in the mysterious sable curtain which covered the bulkhead.

"Hoskins."

No answer.

Paresi put his hand on Hoskins's shoulder. Hoskins's head came up slowly. He did not turn it. His gaze was straight ahead into the darkness. But at least it was off the board.

"Hoskins," said Paresi, "why are you playing chess?"

"Chess is chess," said Hoskins quietly. "Chess may symbolize any conflict, but it is chess and it will remain chess."

"Who are you playing with?"

No answer.

"Hoskins—we need you. Help us."

Hoskins let his gaze travel slowly downward again until it was on the board. "The word is not the thing," he said. "The number is not the thing. The picture, the ideograph, the symbol—these are not the thing. Conversely . . ."

"Yes, Hoskins."

Paresi waited. Hoskins did not move or speak. Paresi put his hand on the man's shoulder again, but now there was no response. He cursed suddenly, bent, and brought up his hand with a violent smash and sent board and pieces flying.

When the clatter had died down Hoskins said pleasantly, "The pieces are not the game. The symbols are not the thing." He sat still, his eyes fixed on the empty chair where the board had been. He put out a hand and moved a piece, where there was no piece, to a square which was no longer there. Then he sat and waited.

Paresi, breathing heavily, backed off, whirled, and went back to the Captain.

Anderson looked up at him, and there was the glimmer of humor in his eyes. "Better sit down and talk about something different, Doctor."

Paresi made an animal sound, soft and deep, far back in his throat, plumped down next to the Captain, and kneaded his hands together for a moment. Then he smiled. "Quite right, Skipper. I'd better."

They sat quietly for a moment. Then the Captain prompted, "About the different breaking points . . ."

"Yes, Captain?"

"Perhaps you can put your finger on the thing that makes different men break in different ways, for different reasons. I mean, Johnny's case seemed pretty clear cut, and what you haven't explained about Hoskins, Hoskins has demonstrated pretty clearly. About Ives, now—we can skip that for the time he'll be unconscious. But if you can figure out where you and I might break, why—we'd know what to look for."

"You think that would help?"

"We'd be prepared."

Paresi looked at him sharply. "Let's hypothesize a child who is afraid of the dark. Ask him and he might say that there's a *something* in dark places that will jump out at him. Then assure him, with great authority, that not only is he right but that it's about to jump any minute, and what have you done?"

"Damage," nodded the Captain. "But you wouldn't say that to the child. You'd tell him there was nothing there. You'd *prove* there wasn't."

"So I would," agreed the Doctor. "But in our case I couldn't do anything of the kind. Johnny broke over machines that really didn't work. Hoskins broke over phenomena that couldn't be measured nor understood. Ives broke over things that scuttled and crawled. Subjectively real phenomena, all of them. Whatever basic terrors hide in you and in me will come to face us, no matter how improbable they might be. And you want me to tell you what they are. No, Skipper. Better leave them in your subconscious, where you've buried them."

"I'm not afraid," said the Captain. "Tell me, Paresi! At least I'll know. I'd rather know. I'd so *damn* much rather know!"

"You're sure I can tell you?"

"Yes."

"I haven't psychoanalyzed you, you know. Some of these things are very hard to—"

"You do know, don't you?"

"Damn you, yes!" Paresi wet his lips. "All right, then. I

may be doing a wrong thing here . . . You've cuddled up to
the idea that I'm a very astute character who automatically
knows about things like this, and it's been a comfort to you.
Well, I've got news for you. I didn't figure all these things
out. I was told."

"Told?"

"Yes, told," said Paresi angrily. "Look, this is supposed to
be restricted information, but the Exploration Service doesn't
rely on individual aptitude tests alone to make up a crew.
There's another factor—call it an inaptitude factor. In its
simplest terms, it comes to this: that a crew can't work together only if each member is the most efficient at his job. He
has to *need* the others, each one of the others. And the word
need predicates *lack*. In other words, none of us is a balanced
individual. And the imbalances are chosen to match and
blend, so that we will react as a balanced unit. Sure I know
Johnny's bugaboos, and Hoskins's, and yours. They were all
in my indoctrination treatments. I know all your case histories, all your psychic push-buttons."

"And yours?" demanded the Captain.

"Hoskins, for example," said Paresi. "Happily married, no
children. Physically inferior all his life. Repressed desire for
pure science, which produced more than a smattering of a
great many sciences and made him a hell of an Engineer.
High idealistic quotient; self sacrifice. Look at him playing
chess, making of this very real situation a theoretical abstraction . . . like leaving a marriage for deep space.

"Johnny we know about. Brought up with never-failing
machines. Still plays with them as if they were toys, and like
any imaginative child, turns to his toys for reassurance. He
needs to be a hero, hence the stars . . .

"Ives . . . always fat. Learned to be easy-going, learned to
laugh *with* when others were laughing *at,* and bottling up
pressures every time it happened. A large appetite. He's here
to satisfy it; he's with us so he can eat up the galaxies . . ."

There was a long pause. "Go on," said the Captain.
"Who's next? You?"

"You," said the Doctor shortly. "You grew up with a burning curiosity about the nature of things. But it wasn't a scien-

tist's curiosity; it was an aesthete's. You're one of the few people alive who refused a subsidized education and worked your way through advanced studies as a crewman on commercial space-liners. You became one of the youngest professors of philosophy in recent history. You made a romantic marriage and your wife died in childbirth. Since then—almost a hundred missions with E.A.S., refusing numerous offers of advancement. Do I have to tell you what your bugaboo is now?"

"No," said Anderson hoarsely. "But I'm . . . not afraid of it. I had no idea your . . ." He swallowed. ". . . information was that complete."

"I wish it wasn't. I wish I had some things to—wonder about," said Paresi with surprising bitterness.

The Captain looked at him shrewdly. "Go on with your case histories."

"I've finished."

"No you haven't." When Paresi did not answer, the Captain nudged him. "Johnny, Ives, Hoskins, me. Haven't you forgotten someone?"

"No I haven't," snarled Paresi, "and if you expect me to tell you why a psychologist buries himself in the stars, I'm not going to do it."

"I don't want to be told anything so general," said the Captain. "I just want to know why *you* came out here."

Paresi scowled. The Captain looked away from him and hazarded, "Big frog in a small pond, Nick?"

Paresi snorted.

Anderson asked, "Women don't like you, do they, Nick?"

Almost inaudibly, Paresi said, "Better cut it out, Skipper."

Anderson said, "Closest thing to being a mother—is that it?"

Paresi went white.

The Captain closed his eyes, frowned, and at last said, "Or maybe you just want to play God."

"I'm going to make it tough for you," said Paresi between his teeth. "There are several ways you can break, just as there are several ways to break a log—explode it, crush it, saw it, burn it . . . One of the ways is to fight me until you win. Me,

because there's no one else left to fight you. So—I won't fight
with you. And you're too rational to attack me unless I do.
That is the thing that will make it tough. If you must break,
it'll have to be some other way."

"Is that what I'm doing?" the Captain asked with sudden
mildness. "I didn't know that. I thought I was trying to get
your own case history out of you, that's all. What are you staring at?"

"Nothing."

There was nothing. Where there had been forward viewports, there was nothing. Where there had been controls, the
communication station, the forward acceleration panels, and
storage lockers; the charts and computers and radar gear—
there was nothing. Blackness; featureless, silent, impenetrable. They sat on one couch by one wall, to which was fixed
one table. Around them was empty floor and a blackness. The
chess player faced into it, and perhaps he was partly within it;
it was difficult to see.

The Captain and the medical officer stared at one another.
There seemed to be nothing to say.

VI

*For man's sense is falsely asserted to be the standard of
things: on the contrary, all the perceptions, both of the senses
and the mind, bear reference to man and not to the universe;
and the human mind resembles those uneven mirrors which
impart their own properties to different objects . . . and dis-
torts and disfigures them . . . For every one . . . has a cave
or den of his own which refracts and discolors the light of nature.*

—*Sir Francis Bacon*
(1561—1626)

It was the Captain who moved first. He went to the remaining bulkhead, spun a dog, and opened a cabinet. From it
he took a rack of spare radar parts and three thick coils of
wire. Paresi, startled, turned and saw Hoskins peering owlishly at the Captain.

Anderson withdrew some tools, reached far back in the
cabinet, and took out a large bottle.

"Oh," said Paresi. "That. . . . I thought you were doing something constructive."

In the far shadows, Hoskins turned silently back to his game. The Captain gazed down at the bottle, tossed it, caught it. "I am," he said. "I am."

He came and sat beside the Doctor. He thumbed off the stopper and drank ferociously. Paresi watched, his eyes as featureless as the imprisoning dark.

"Well?" said the Captain pugnaciously.

Paresi's hands rose and fell, once. "Just wondering why."

"Why I'm going to get loopin', stoopin' drunk? I'll tell you why, head-shrinker. Because I want to, that's why. Because I like it. I'm doing something I like because I like it. I'm not doing it because of the inversion of this concealed repression as expressed in the involuted feelings my childhood developed in my attitude toward the sex life of beavers, see, couch-catechizer old boy? I like it and that's why."

"I knew a man who went to bed with old shoes because he liked it," said Paresi coldly.

The Captain drank again and laughed harshly. "Nothing can change you, can it, Nick?"

Paresi looked around him almost fearfully. "I can change," he whispered. "Ives is gone. Give me the bottle."

Something clattered to the deck at the hem of the black curtain.

" 'S another hallucination," said the Captain. "Go pick up the hallucination, Nicky boy."

"Not my hallucination," said Paresi. "Pick it up yourself."

"Sure," said the Captain good-naturedly. He waited while Paresi drank, took back the bottle, tilted it sharply over his mouth. He wiped his lips with the back of his hand, exhaled heavily, and went to the blackness across the cabin.

"Well, what do you know," he breathed.

"What is it this time?"

Anderson held the thing up. "A trophy, that's what." He peered at it. "*All-American 2675*. Little statue of a guy holding up a victory wreath. Nice going, little guy." He strode to Paresi and snatched away the bottle. He poured liquor on the head of the figurine. "Have a drink, little guy."

"Let me see that."

Paresi took it, held it, turned it over. Suddenly he dropped it as if it were a red-hot coal. "Oh, dear God . . ."

" 'Smatter, Nick?" The Captain picked up the statuette and peered at it.

"Put it down, put it down," said the Doctor in a choked voice. "It's—Johnny . . ."

"Oh, it is, it is," breathed the Captain. He put down the statuette gingerly on the table, hesitated, then turned its face away from them. With abrupt animation he swung to Paresi. "Hey! You didn't say it looked like Johnny. You said it *was* Johnny!"

"Did I?"

"Yup." He grinned wolfishly. "Not bad for a psychologist. What a peephole you opened up! Graven images, huh?"

"Shut up, Anderson," said Paresi tiredly. "I told you I'm not going to let you needle me."

"Aw now, it's all in fun," said the Captain. He plumped down and threw a heavy arm across Paresi's shoulders. "Le's be friends. Le's sing a song."

Paresi shoved him away. "Leave me alone. Leave me alone."

Anderson turned away from him and regarded the statuette gravely. He extended the bottle toward it, muttered a greeting, and drank. "I wonder . . ."

The words hung there until Paresi twisted up out of his forlorn reverie to bat them down. "Damn it—*what* do you wonder?"

"Oh," said the Captain jovially, "I was just wondering what you'll be."

"What are you talking about?"

Anderson waved the bottle at the figurine, which called it to his attention again, and so again he drank. "Johnny turned into what he thinks he is. A little guy with a big victory. Hoskins, there, he's going to be a slide-rule, jus' you wait and see. Ol' Ives, that's easy. He's going to be a beer barrel, with beer in it. Always did have a head on him, Ives did." He stopped to laugh immoderately at Paresi's darkening face. "Me, I have no secrets no more. I'm going to be a coat of arms—a useless philosophy rampant on a field of stars." He put the open mouth of the bottle against his forehead and pressed it violently, lowered it, and touched the angry red ring it left between his eyes. "Mark of the beast," he confided. "Caste mark. Zero, that's me and my whole damn family. The die is cast, the caste has died." He grunted appreciatively and turned again to Paresi. "But what's old Nicky going to be?"

"Don't call me Nicky," said the Doctor testily.

"I know," said the Captain, narrowing his eyes and laying one finger alongside his nose. "A ref'rence book, tha's what you'll be. A treatise on the . . . the post-nasal hysterectomy, or how to unbutton a man's prejudices and take down his pride . . . I swiped all that from somewhere . . .

"No!" he shouted suddenly; then, with conspiratorial quiet, he said, "You won't be no book, Nicky boy. Covers aren't hard enough. Not the right type face. Get it?" he roared, and dug Paresi viciously in the ribs. "Type face, it's a witticism."

Paresi bent away from the blow like a caterpillar being bitten by a fire-ant. He said nothing.

"And finally," said the Captain, "you won't be a book because you got   no   spine." He leapt abruptly to his feet. "Well, what do you know!"

He bent and scooped up an unaccountable object that rested by the nearest shadows. It was a quarter-keg of beer.

He hefted it and thumped it heavily down on the table. "Come on, Nick," he chortled. "Gather ye round. Here's old Ives, like I said."

Paresi stared at the keg, his eyes stretched so wide open that the lids moved visibly with his pulse. "Stop it, Anderson, you swine . . ."

The Captain tossed him a disgusted glance and a matching snort. From the clutter of radar gear he pulled a screwdriver and a massive little step-down transformer down on its handle. The bung disappeared explosively inside the keg and was replaced by a gout of white foam. Paresi shrieked.

"Ah, shaddup," growled Anderson. He rummaged until he

found a tube-shield. He stripped off a small length of self-welding metal tape and clapped it over the terminal-hole at the closed end of the shield, making it into an adequate mug. He waited a moment while the weld cooled, then tipped the keg until solid beer began to run with the foam. He filled the improvised mug and extended it toward Paresi.

"Good ol' Ives," he said sentimentally. "Come on, Paresi. Have a drink on Ives."

Paresi turned and covered his face like a frightened woman.

Anderson shrugged and drank the beer. "It's good beer," he said. He glanced down at the Doctor, who suddenly flung himself face down across the couch with his head hanging out of sight on the opposite side, from which came the sounds of heaving and choking.

"Poor ol' Nick," said the Captain sadly. He refilled the mug and sat down. With his free hand he patted Paresi's back. "Can't take it. Poor, poor ol' Nick . . ."

After that there was a deepening silence, a deepening blackness. Paresi was quiet now, breathing very slowly, holding each breath, expelling air and lying quiet for three full seconds before each inhalation, as if breathing were a conscious effort—more; as if breathing were the whole task, the entire end of existence. Anderson slumped lower and lower. Each time he blinked his lids opened a fraction less, while the time his eyes stayed closed became a fraction of a second longer. The cabin waited as tensely as the taut pose of the rigid little victory trophy.

Then there was the music.

It was soft, grand music; the music of pageantry, cloth-of-gold and scarlet vestments; pendant jewels and multicolored dimness shouldering upward to be lost in vaulted stone. It was music which awaited the accompaniment of whispers, thousands of awed, ritualistic sibilants which would carry no knowable meaning and only one avowed purpose. Soft music, soft, soft; not soft as to volume, for the volume grew and grew, but soft with the softness of clouds which are soft for all their mountain-size and brilliance; soft and living as a tiger's throat, soft as a breast, soft as the act of drowning, and huge as a cloud.

Anderson made two moves: he raised his head, and he spun the beer in his mug so its center surface sank and the bubbles whirled. With his head up and his eyes down, he sat watching the bubbles circle and slow.

Paresi rose slowly and went to the center of the small lighted space left to them, and slowly he knelt. His arms came up and out, and his upturned face was twisted and radiant.

Before him in the blackness there was—or perhaps there had been for some time—a blue glow, almost as lightless as the surrounding dark, but blue and physically deep for all that. Its depth increased rather than its light. It became the ghost of a grotto, the mouth of a nameless Place.

And in it was a person. A . . . *presence*. It beckoned.

Paresi's face gleamed wetly. "Me?" he breathed. "You want—me?"

It beckoned.

"I—don't believe you," said Paresi. "You can't want me. You don't know who I am. You don't know what I am, what I've done. You don't want me . . ." His voice quavered almost to inaudibility " do you?"

It beckoned.

"Then you know," sang Paresi in the voice of revelation. "I have denied you with my lips, but you know, you know, you know that underneath . . . deep down . . . I have not wavered for an instant. I have kept your image before me."

He rose. Now Anderson watched him.

"You are my life," said Paresi, "my hopes, my fulfillment. You are all wisdom and all charity. Thank you, thank you . . . Master. I give thee thanks, oh Lord," he blurted, and walked straight into the blue glow.

There was an instant when the music was an anthem, and then it too was gone.

Anderson's breath whistled out. He lifted his beer, checked himself, then set it down gently by the figurine of the athlete. He went to the place where Paresi had disappeared, bent, and picked up a small object. He swore, and came back to the couch.

He sucked his thumb and swore again. "Your thorns are sharp, Paresi."

Carefully he placed the object between the beer keg and the statuette. It was a simple wooden cross. Around the arms and shaft, twisted tightly and biting deeply into the wood, was a thorny withe. "God all mighty, Nick," Anderson said mournfully, "you didn't have to hide it. Nobody'd have minded."

"Well?" he roared suddenly at the blackness, "What are you waiting for? Am I in your way? Have I done anything to stop you? Come on, come on!"

His voice rebounded from the remaining bulkhead, but was noticeably swallowed up in the absorbent blackness. He waited until its last reverberations had died, and then until its memory was hard to fix. He pounded futilely at the couch cushions, glared all about in a swift, intense, animal way. Then he relaxed, bent down, and fumbled for the alcohol bottle. "What's the matter with you, out there?" he demanded quietly. "You waiting for me to sober up? You want me to be myself before you fix me up? You want to know something? *In vino veritas,* that's what. You don't have to wait for me, kiddies. I'm a hell of a lot more me right now than I will be after I get over this." He took the figurine and replaced it on the other side of the keg. "Tha's right, Johnny. Get over on the other side of ol' Beer-belly there. Make room for the old man." To the blackness he said, "Look, I got neat habits, don't leave me on no deck, hear? Rack me up alongside the boys. What is it I'm going to be? Oh yeah. A coat of arms. Hey, I forgot the motto. All righty: this is my motto. '*Sic itur ad astra*'—that is to say, 'This is the way to the men's room.' "

Somewhere a baby cried.

Anderson threw his forearm over his eyes.

Someone went "Shh!" but the baby went right on crying.

Anderson said, "Who's there?"

"Just me, darling."

He breathed deeply, twice, and then whispered, "Louise?"

"Of course. *Shh,* Jeannie!"

"Jeannie's with you, Louise? She's all right? You're—all

right?"

"Come and see," the sweet voice chuckled.

Captain Anderson dove into the blackness aft. It closed over him silently and completely.

On the table stood an ivory figurine, a quarter-keg of beer, a thorny cross, and a heart. It wasn't a physiological specimen; rather it was the archetype of the most sentimental of symbols; the balanced, cushiony, brilliant-red valentine heart. Through it was a golden arrow, and on it lay cut flowers: lilies, white roses, and forget-me-nots. The heart pulsed strongly; and though it pumped no blood, at least it showed that it was alive, which made it, perhaps, a better thing than it looked at first glance.

Now it was very quiet in the ship, and very dark.

VII

. . . *We are about to land. The planet is green and blue below us, and the long trip is over. . . . It looks as if it might be a pleasant place to live . . .*

A fragment of Old Testament verse has been running through my mind—from Ecclesiastes, I think. I don't remember it verbatim, but it's something like this:

To every thing there is a season, and a time to every purpose under heaven: A time to weep, and a time to laugh; a time to mourn, and a time to dance; A time to get, and a time to lose; a time to keep, and a time to cast away; A time to be born, and a time to die; a time to plant, and a time to pluck up that which is planted.

For me, anyway, I feel that the time has come. Perhaps it is not to die, but something else, less final or more terrible.

In any case, you will remember, I know, what we decided long ago—that a man owes one of two things to his planet, to his race: posterity, or himself. I could not contribute the first —it is only proper that I should offer the second and not shrink if it is accepted . . .

—From a letter by Peter Hoskins to his wife.

In the quiet and the dark, Hoskins moved.

"Checkmate," he said.

He rose from his chair and crossed the cabin. Ignoring

what was on the table, he opened a drawer under the parts cabinet and took out a steel rule. From a book rack he lifted down a heavy manual. He sat on the end of the couch with the manual on his knees and leafed through it, smoothing it open at a page of physical measurements. He glanced at the floor, across it to the black curtain, back to the one exposed bulkhead. He grunted, put the book down, and carried his tape to the steel wall. He anchored one end of it there by flipping the paramagnetic control on the tape case, and pulled the tape across the room. At the blackness he took a reading, made a mark.

Then he took a fore-and-aft measurement from a point opposite the forward end of the table to one opposite the after end of the bunk. Working carefully, he knelt and constructed a perpendicular to this line. He put the tape down for the third time, arriving again at the outboard wall of darkness. He stood regarding it thoughtfully, and then unhesitatingly plunged his arm into it. He fumbled for a moment, moving his hand around in a circle, pressing forward, trying again. Suddenly there was a click, a faint hum. He stepped back.

Something huge shouldered out of the dark. It pressed forward toward him, passed him, stopped moving.

It was the port.

Hoskins wiped sweat away from his upper lip and stood blinking into the airlock until the outer port opened as well. Warm afternoon sunlight and a soft, fresh breeze poured in. In the wind was birdsong and the smell of growing things. Hoskins gazed into it, his mild eyes misty. Then he turned back to the cabin.

The darkness was gone. Ives was sprawled on the after couch, apparently unconscious. Johnny was smiling in his sleep. The Captain was snoring stertorously, and Paresi was curled up like a cat on the floor. The sunlight streamed in through the forward viewports. The manual wheel gleamed on the bulkhead, unbroken.

Hoskins looked at the sleeping crew and shook his head, half-smiling. Then he stepped to the control console and lifted a microphone from its hook. He began to speak softly into it in his gentle, unimpressive voice. He said:

"Reality is what it is, and not what it seems to be. What it seems to be is an individual matter, and even in the individual it varies constantly. If that's a truism, it's still the truth, as true as the fact that this ship cannot fail. The course of events after our landing would have been profoundly different if we had unanimously accepted the thing we knew to be true. But none of us need feel guilty on that score. We are not conditioned to deny the evidence of our senses.

"What the natives of this planet have done is, at base, simple and straightforward. They had to know if the race who built this ship could do so because they were psychologically sound (and therefore capable of reasoning out the building process, among many, many other things) or whether we were merely mechanically apt. To find this out, they tested us. They tested us the way we test steel—to find out its breaking point. And while they were playing a game for our sanity, I played a game for our lives. I could not share it with any of you because it was a game only I, of us all, have experience in. Paresi was right to a certain degree when he said I had retreated into abstraction—the abstraction of chess. He was wrong, though, when he concluded I had been driven to it. You can be quite sure that I did it by choice. It was simply a matter of translating the contactual evidence into an equivalent idea-system.

"I learned very rapidly that when they play a game, they abide by the rules. I know the rules of chess, but I did not know the rules of their game. They did not give me their rules. They simply permitted me to convey mine to them.

"I learned a little more slowly that, though their power to reach our minds is unheard-of in any of the seven galaxies we know about, it still cannot take and use any but the ideas in the fore-front of our consciousness. In other words, chess was a possibility. They could be forced to take a sacrificed piece, as well as being forced to lose one of their own. They extrapolate a sequence beautifully—but they can be outthought. So much for that: I beat them at chess. And by confining my efforts to the chessboard, where I knew the rules and where they respected them, I was able to keep what we

call sanity. Where you were disturbed because the port disappeared, I was not disturbed because the disappearance was
not chess.

"You're wondering, of course, how they did what they did
to us. I don't know. But I can tell you what they did. They
empathize—that is, see through our eyes, feel with our fingertips—so that they perceive what we do. Second, they can
control those perceptions; hang on a distortion circuit, as Ives
would put it, between the sense organ and the brain. For example, you'll find all our fingerprints all around the port control, where, one after the other, we punched the wall and
thought we were punching the button.

"You're wondering, too, what I did to break their hold on
us. Well, I simply believed what I knew to be the truth; that
the ship is unharmed and unchanged. I measured it with a
steel tape and it was so. Why didn't they force me to misread
the tape? They would have, if I'd done that measuring first.
At the start they were in the business of turning every piece of
pragmatic evidence into an outright lie. But I outlasted the
test. When they'd finished with their whole arsenal of sensory
lies, they still hadn't broken me. They then turned me loose,
like a rat in a maze, to see if I could find the way out. And
again they abided by their rules. They didn't change the
maze when at last I attacked it.

"Let me rephrase what I've done; I feel uncomfortable cast
as a superman. We five pedestrians faced some heavy traffic on a surface road. You four tried nobly to cross—deaf and
blind-folded. You were all casualties. I was not; and it wasn't
because I am stronger or wiser than you, but only because I
stayed on the sidewalk and waited for the light to
change. . . .

"So we won. Now . . ."

Hoskins paused to wet his lips. He looked at his shipmates,
each in turn, each for a long, reflective moment. Again his
gentle face showed the half-smile, the small shake of the
head. He lifted the mike.

". . .In my chess game I offered them a minor piece in
order to achieve a victory, and they accepted. My interpreta-
tion is that they want *me* for further tests. This need not con-

cern you on either of the scores which occur to you as you hear this. First: The choice is my own. It is not a difficult one to make. As Paresi once pointed out, I have a high idealistic quotient. Second: I am, after all, a very minor piece and the game is a great one. I am convinced that there is no test to which they can now subject me, and break me, that any one of you cannot pass.

"But you must in no case come tearing after me in a wild and thoughtless rescue attempt. I neither want that nor need it. And do not judge the natives severely; we are in no position to do so. I am certain now that whether I come back or not, these people will make a valuable addition to the galactic community.

"Good luck, in any case. If the tests shouldn't prove too arduous, I'll see you again. If not, my only regret is that I shall break up what has turned out to be, after all, a very effective team. If this happens, tell my wife the usual things and deliver to her a letter you will find among my papers. She was long ago reconciled to eventualities.

"Johnny . . . the natives will fix your lighter . . .

"Good luck, good-bye."

Hoskins hung up the microphone. He took a stylus and wrote a line: "*Hear my recording. Pete.*"

And then, bareheaded and unarmed, he stepped through the port, out into the golden sunshine. Outside he stopped, and for a moment touched his cheek to the flawless surface of the hull.

He walked down into the valley.

2. *A Monster Named Smith*

PANIC! ISOLATION! TERROR!

Blind, mindless, insensate. Odorless, dumb, deaf. Fear.

Pressure from within, instinctive and powerful. Around it, a constriction. Cause unknown. Conflict. Pain.

One sense remains. Listen! Send out feelers through the darkness! Somewhere there must be something else alive. Somewhere there is a reason for fear. Listen!

"The board shows a gap on Harrison. If open, detail a company to close it up. General orders to all searching parties: every building will be thoroughly searched, inside and out, top to bottom. Search everything, in, under, above. Parties will not proceed until certain that every building is clear, every eave and rooftop is clean."

"Is that right, Mr. Gardner?"

"Don't ask me," Gardner snapped. "Mr. Burke is in charge here." He turned to Burke. "As city manager, I can't permit the city to be shut down undefinitely on mere suspicion. Besides the personal distress and inconvenience, this shutdown is costing the city millions of dollars an hour . . ."

"Would you rather be a zombi—you and all the other millions of people in the city?"

"You have a wild imagination. You don't *know* that the thing can take over a man. You aren't even sure that it escaped. And if something did escape, you can't be sure it's still alive. There was no reason for the declaration of martial law."

"I'll give you a reason," Burke explained quietly. "The animal is dead. Cold, stony. No doubt about it. The deceleration killed it. With extraterrestrial fauna, we have to work fast. We can't be sure how soon decomposition will set in or how the internal organs will be affected. The body is in the examination room, on the dissecting table, within minutes after landing. But before we can make an incision, something starts oozing out from under it. A black blob . . ."

"Good God! What's that?" Daniels was more startled than afraid. He was staring at the sheep-like animal on the dissecting table. The scalpel was poised in his hand.

Burke was afraid. He had been afraid for a long time. "Parasite," he said. He spat it out viciously, as if that would deny his fear.

The inky blob continued to ooze.

Ellis, who had insisted, like Burke, on being present as an observer, was calm and analytical as usual. "Not necessarily," he said. "Could be a symbiosis."

"Symbiosis is a careful balance," Burke said violently. "For us it's a parasite. Dangerous. What I was afraid of all along."

"Okay, okay," Daniels put in quickly. "The question is, what do we do with it?"

"Kill it!"

"How?"

"Not so fast," Ellis said. "We can't be sure it's dangerous. This opportunity *might* be unique."

"It took over this thing," Burke pointed out. "It's an animal, like us. We can't take the chance that it could adapt itself to man."

The blob oozed. It was bigger than a hand, now.

"It has to have a means of propagation," Burke said, suppressing a shudder. "It's amorphous, like an amoeba. Binary fission is indicated. If so, then no one on Earth is safe. We shouldn't have brought it back."

The blob oozed. It was the size of a dinner plate. It had begun to thin out near the body.

Ellis sighed. "Kill it."

Daniels sliced down with the scalpel in his hand. It passed effortlessly through the blob, as if through a shadow, and skidded along the stainless steel top of the table. The blob, uncut, continued to pull itself free of the animal.

It was like a pool of ink. There was no smell to it and maybe no feel either, but no one offered to touch it. It was just black. Innocent, maybe, but black and alien and therefore evil.

Daniels was shaken. Without reason.

"Obviously it can't be cut or shot or hurt by any such weapon," Burke said impatiently.

"Well, do something," Daniels stammered. "Don't just stand there talking about it. It's pulling itself free. It'll be coming after one of us in a minute."

Ellis glanced around the room. "The door's closed. Nobody leaves here."

"What good will that do," Daniels objected strenuously, "if it can interpenetrate matter?"

"Flesh and steel are two different substances. It hasn't entered the table."

"You mean we're stuck here with that thing until it gets us or we can find a way to kill it?" Daniels shouted.

Ellis nodded impatiently. "Obviously." He studied the room again. "Somewhere within these walls we have to find a weapon or a poison."

By now Burke had collected a litter of bottles from the reagent cabinet. He tried them on the blob. Acids and bases, one by one they poured into the blackness and fumed together and dripped onto the floor to eat holes in the rubberized covering. The body of the animal began to dissolve in the growing puddle on the table. The stench of the chemicals and their reactions was almost stifling. Nobody seemed to notice.

The blob pulled and thinned and grew larger and remained unaltered by the chemicals. Burke looked around hastily. He grabbed up a burner, turned it on, lit it. It burned blue and hot.

He held it upside down, pointed toward the black pool. The blob squirmed. Burke pressed the burner close. The blob moved quickly, moved away from the flame, and as it moved, the last strand of blackness pulled loose from the dissolving, alien body.

"Quick!" Daniels said hysterically. "Before it gets away!

It's afraid of the fire!"

Burke hadn't waited. He held the flame as close to the blob as he could get it. "We need a blow-torch," he said.

The blob squirmed. It flowed away from the flame, across the table, and the flame looked as if it turned back from the blackness. But it wasn't that. There just wasn't enough gas pressure. The flame curled up naturally.

The darkness wavered, its edges curling. It wriggled and began to flap, first one side and then the other, alternating. Slowly, awkwardly, it began to fly. It climbed into the air and circled around the room silently, a blot of darkness.

"Close the ventilators!" Ellis said quickly.

Burke raced to the side of the room and pulled the switch that slipped steel shutters across the gratings.

"Oh God, oh God!" Daniels was saying. He cringed beside the table, shaking, as the blackness swooped close.

"The interpenetration is obviously variable," Ellis said. "Otherwise it couldn't fly."

"Or the only thing it can penetrate is flesh," Burke amended. He was searching the room for another weapon, futilely.

The circular shadow flapped its way high into one corner of the room. It pressed itself against the ceiling and clung, unmoving. It looked like a black stain. They stared up at it, the three of them, with different eyes. Ellis was curious; Burke was murderous; Daniels was terror-stricken.

Daniels moved.

"Stay away from that door!" Ellis snapped.

Daniels stopped. He was shaking as he looked back over his shoulder. "We can't kill it," he said. His voice shook, too. "What do we do? Wait here until it decides which one of us it wants?"

"If we have to," Ellis said.

"The question is, how long can it live outside a host?" Burke said. "It isn't breathing. Presumably, it can't eat in its present form. But it does use up energy. If we can't kill it, we can starve it to death."

"Unless we starve first," Daniels moaned.

"We'll run out of air before then," Ellis observed.

"We'll have to take a chance. One of us will leave for a

blow-torch," Burke said.

"Me!" Daniels panted. "Me!"

"I'm staying here," Burke said. "I don't want to let it out of my sight. You're staying here, too, Daniels. We want someone who will come back." He looked at Ellis; Ellis nodded. "I'll stand guard in front of the door with the burner. If you open the door just a crack, you can slip through before it can move."

Daniels was standing by the table where the animal was half-dissolved. His eyes were wild and staring.

The burner hose wouldn't reach to the door. Burke pulled off his shirt, looked at Ellis, who was standing beside the door, and held his shirt close to the flame. The shirt smoked and started to burn. In two quick steps Burke was in front of the door, his back to it, his eyes on the blot of darkness that clung to the ceiling.

"Go!" he said.

Ellis moved. And the blot moved, swooping down at Burke. Burke waved the flaming shirt. The door behind him slipped open. The blot swerved in the air, away from the flames. It headed straight for Daniels. Daniels screamed. He put his arms around his head and sprinted blindly for the door.

The blot followed him, only a foot behind. Burke glanced at them, at Daniels and the blot, and he tried to do two things at once. He lowered his shoulder at Daniels and tossed the burning shirt at the blot. Somehow, both missed. Daniels sidestepped instinctively, and the blot swerved in the air.

Flesh smacked solidly against flesh. Something snapped. As Burke spun around, he caught a glimpse of the blot slipping through the door. Daniels was gone.

"Commander!" Burke gasped. "What happened?"

Ellis raised a white face from the floor. "Broken leg," he said, and fainted.

Burke turned and ran toward the intercom. "Air lock guard," he snapped. "Close the lock. Emergency."

Trained responses were quick. No one questioned orders like that. Burke heard the whirring of motors. Something clanged shut, with finality.

"What's up?" asked a tinny voice.

"Anything get out that lock in the last second or two?"
Burke asked quickly.

"Nobody."

"Anything, I said!"

"Well, no—I mean—I don't think so. I had a feeling that
something brushed past me like—like—"

"Like what?"

"Well, like a bat. Only it wasn't a bat. What's going on
anyway?"

"Hell to pay! Com room! Com room! Put the radar on a
small object, about the size of a bird, flying out from the ship!
Whatever you do, don't lose it! Then get Washington. Secspace. I'll be there in five seconds. Doc! To the examination
room on the double. Commander's got a broken leg. And
send two men to pick up Daniels and hold him for observa-
tion. He's hysterical. Leaving now for the Com room. Off!"

Shock! Identity!
Terror! Conflict! Pain! Isolation!
We are one. Once we were many. Remember. Remember!

The object falling from the sky, gleaming in the sunlight,
gleam dimmed by a shortening leg of flame.
Scatter, brothers!
Much later, the object opening a mouth, black against the
shiny skin. Is the object hungry?
Run, brothers!
Things coming out, climbing down, standing on the
ground, two-legged, tall. Beings.
Listen, brothers!

"Sheep! I'll be damned. Nothing but sheep!"

"Don't be fooled. They're more than sheep."

"Well, look at them. What would you call them?"

"Yes, look at them. See them standing there looking at us,
as if they could understand everything we say."

"Now, Burke, don't let your imagination run away with
you. I agree, it's unlikely that they're identical with our Earth
sheep, but they look like them and we might as well call them

that."

"It's a dangerous mental trick, Commander. We delude ourselves into thinking we understand them when we give them a name."

"Maybe they look to you like they're listening to us, but my guess is that it's curiosity. After all, we're the only other beings they've ever seen."

"That's just it. Where's the rest of the fauna? We've scouted every land mass, and these are the only animals we've seen. How do you account for that?"

"Why should we have to?"

"Oh, God preserve us!"

"Be a little patient, Burke. We all aren't ecologists. The others may not see what's so obvious to you. What you're trying to say is that evolution wouldn't produce just one species."

"What do you think! Look at this world. As pretty as a spring day. Mild. Gentle. And inhabited by nothing but these herbivores. And not very many of them, either."

"I've seen plenty of them."

"Not under the circumstances."

"And you think these sheep wiped out all the rest of the fauna?"

"Obviously."

"It could have been natural conditions."

"That destroyed everything but these things? Nonsense."

"Well, then, they wiped out the rest. So what?"

"How? Man has been top dog on Earth for a long, long time, and we haven't even come close to wiping out our pests and carnivores. As bloodthirsty as we are. What does that make these things? It makes them the most deadly creatures we've ever known."

"These sheep? Nuts!"

"It is a little farfetched, Burke."

"Think of this, then. What keeps their numbers down? With all this grazing land available, there's only a fraction of the number of these creatures that there should be. With no natural enemies, with nothing to prey on them, according to Malthusian law they should expand in the presence of abundant food to the limit of the land to feed them, and a little beyond. Like the rabbits in Australia. Or man himself."

"Maybe their natural enemies are small. Insects. Germs and viruses. Or maybe they're almost sterile."

"And maybe they control their breeding. Or maybe it's controlled for them. That's something we've never been able to do. That frightens me more than the other."

"You've just set foot on this world and you're frightened already. What will you be like before we're ready to leave?"

"Gibbering. You think that's funny, but a sensible man knows when to be frightened. I'm afraid now."

Hosts! The thought was startling and puzzled. *Hosts, brothers, without directors! Self-directed hosts that have come from a long way off in that thing they call a ship, from the nightlights, where all are like they are. Danger!*

Later. Much later.

"I guess we're done. The mapping is finished. The ship is crammed with samples of everything we could lay our hands on. The really thorough analysis will have to wait until we get back to Earth. But from our investigations we can report that the expedition exceeded our fondest hopes. I don't see why colonization can't begin immediately. We take off tomorrow."

"Samples of everything? You've forgotten one. We haven't any sheep."

"Haven't seen any for weeks. They've disappeared. Just after Daniels decided he wanted one for dissection."

"Doesn't that seem significant to you?"

"Now, Burke. Let's not get started on that again."

"I suggest we put out traps tonight. I don't feel that this survey is complete when we don't have any specimens of the dominant form of life. *The* form of life, for that matter."

"No! I don't agree. Taking back specimens before we understand them would be incredibly dangerous. We don't know anything about them. Give them a chance to get loose on Earth, and we might have the story of the rabbits in Australia all over again."

"There's no chance of that, Burke. We aren't going to give them a chance to get loose. And we've seen nothing to indicate that they're dangerous. You've been studying them ever since we landed, and you haven't discovered anything."

"A negative answer that's practically worthless. As you pointed out a moment ago, they all disappeared weeks ago. As long as I don't have answers to the two questions I suggested when we first landed, I must regard them as the most dangerous things we've ever encountered. How did they kill off their competitors? And what controls their breeding?"

"I'm afraid Secspace wouldn't look at it that way. I'm afraid we would be considered derelict in our duties if we returned without a specimen. Although I'll put your protest on record, of course."

"A specimen, you said?"

"All right, Burke. Just one. There can't be any danger of them multiplying. Will that satisfy you?"

"No. We can't be sure that they propagate sexually. Not without dissection which we haven't been able to perform. But if it's the only concession I can get—"

"It is. And you can console yourself with the hope that the traps will be empty tomorrow morning, as they have been every other morning."

A specimen, brothers. One of us. One? What is that? A host and a director. One must go. Or they will return to exterminate us, as we exterminated the others. One must go. Which one? One ready for division. One of us. This part of us. Go.

A belonging. We are not a whole, but a part of. We have a mission.

The pressure from within continues. It is agony, but it is agony located and identified. We must divide. That is it. That is the pressure. We are one. Once we were many. We must be many again.

But there is terror, and while there is terror we cannot divide. Fear is a force that binds us around, that closes us in so tight we cannot divide. We need peace. We must have peace. But we are encircled by enemies who seek to destroy us. They

will destroy us unless we destroy them first. But we are one,
and they are many.

Learn. Learn the dangers of this alien world. Learn the
powers of these alien beings. Learn survival. Back. Back to
the Enemy . . .

"Troops equipped with flame-throwers will lead the advance. They will fire at anything black, any spot, any shadow.
They will fire first and ask questions afterwards."

"Good God, Burke! Don't let that order go out! You don't
know what you're saying. Think what will happen if you tell
soldiers to shoot at *anything!*"

"I'm thinking what will happen if they don't. There
shouldn't be anybody inside that area except the searching
parties. And firemen and equipment are following the soldiers in to put out the fires . . . Air patrol! All flame-thrower-
equipped helicopters will fire at any small flying object, bird
or bat. Particularly bats. They will keep pace with the ground
forces working in."

"But you don't even know that the thing is in the city!"

"We followed it by radar from the ship until we lost it over
the center of the city. By that time the permanent radar in-
stallations around the city were alerted, and we had a line of
helicopters shooting down everything that flies. Radar didn't
pick up a thing. Don't worry, we'll get it. We'll find it and destroy it."

"But will there be anything left when you get through.
You're the kind who would burn down a house to get rid of
termites!"

"Mr. Gardner. City manager or not, one more outburst and
I'll have you ejected from primary control. You're here to
help us with your knowledge of the city, and all I've heard so
far is objections to everything we do."

"Looters, Mr. Burke. Looters reported inside the cordon."

"That area has to be kept clear. The soldiers will shoot
them down on sight. Put that announcement out through
every media, radio, television, loudspeakers. The bodies will
be incinerated where they fall. All animals will receive the
same treatment. Let nothing that moves slip through the cor-

don. . . ."

That is the Enemy. Shrewd and murderous. If we could
only kill him— But there is no chance. He is too well guard-
ed.

We are growing weak. We are not meant for this kind of existence. The escape, the long flight, and now the internal
struggle to divide, stifled by terror, has sapped our strength.
We need food. For that we must have a host. Where are we.
How close are the searchers and their flames?

We are blind without a host. We starve without a host. And
yet we had no choice. We had to leave our old host because it
was dead. We had to leave it to divide. And now there is no
peace, and we cannot divide.

We can kill many of them, but eventually they will destroy
us. We can swoop down on them and touch them with death,
but they would turn their flames upon us, and we would die.
We felt it there in the ship, when the flame was turned toward us. We felt what we had never known before, the possibility of death. We, who are immortal, could die.

Reach out, reach out! Find the searchers! How close are
they? How do they work? Find out, so that we can plan.

We reach. We fumble. We see . . .

The night lit with brief, oily flares that shred the darkness.
The marching ranks, watchful, ready. The machines, rolling,
ponderous. The bright lights that roam ahead and around and
up.

"My God, Joe, look at it! An army! What the hell's it all
for?"

"You know as much as I do. They just turned us out in the
middle of the night and rushed us up here like somebody's
pants was on fire. Look for something! What? Hell, I don't
know. Shoot at anything that moves! Shoot at shadows! With
flame-throwers! Somebody's gone off his nut, I guess."

A shadow leaps in a shielded corner. A nozzle spits greasy,
licking flame. Wood smokes and then burns. A stream of
water hisses on it, turning into steam.

"Halt!"

The marching ranks halt. The machines stop. Only the lights keep moving. 'The helicopters hang motionless in the air above, black nozzles poking out from them like a dragon's smoky nostrils, landing lights burning down onto the roof-tops.

"Company A will take the building to the right. Company B will take the building to the left. They will work their way to the top and onto the roof. From the top-story windows they will look up toward the eaves. Burn anything black, any shadow, anything. Firemen will follow with hand extinguishers. Remaining companies will stay in ranks until the search is completed. Get going!"

Up through the building, searching for shadows. Climbing long steps, peering up and down elevator shafts, inspecting every cranny, drawer, crack. Lifting rugs, turning over furniture, removing cushions. Shooting fire at shadows.

Up and up. Feeling a little silly, but impressed, somehow, by the size of the operation, and the seriousness, and being thorough because the Captain is watching. A shot, below in the street, echoing up. Rush to the window; peer out. A civilian is in the street below, stretched out. You know that he is dead. As you watch, flame blackens the body, eats at it until there is only a cinder.

"What's the matter, boy? Nervous?"

"Hell, yes! Ain't you?"

And eventually you go down and out and the ranks march on a few paces and halt and this time it is your turn to wait in the street while other companies search. In the distance you can see other helicopters hovering, their lights brilliant, a circle of them. The center seems to be the black hulk of the public library . . .

Hopeless! They are all around, these alien killers, these hosts without directors. We are one, and they are many. We despair. We will die here, wherever we are. We can reach out and feel them, closing in upon us from every direction. The circle draws in upon us, nearer, nearer . . .

And someone approaches. We sense the thought, slow and stumbling. It is not one of the searchers. They are still fairly distant. He looks up.

"Public library. Nothing there. Nothing but books. Got to hurry. They'll be here soon. Before that I got to find me a place to sleep or seem like it. They're killing people. Christ!"

A chance, a chance. The thought sings through us like a surge of energy. He is below. We sense him there. That means that we are above him, clinging under the roof of the building he thinks of as the public library.

Will he welcome us or fight? Is he weak or strong? It does not matter. We have no choice. We must take the chance. If we can get nourishment and sight, if we can get outside the searchers, we can reach a place of safety and peace where we can leave him, where we can divide. And it must be soon. He will die, of course, and it is unfortunate. But we have no choice.

Let loose, now. Release our hold. Fall through the air, fluttering at first, then swooping down upon him. We reach out to him, and he suspects nothing. His mind is busy with other things, the things he is looking for, like the things he has hidden in his pockets.

Down upon him. Closer. Slowly now. He feels nothing as we light. His thoughts move on, busy, roiled. Let the probes reach in through the back of the neck, delicately. There!

He stands stiffly, immobile, a scream echoing through his mind, silent, unvoiced. But as we go in, he shrinks back, not fighting, somehow relieved, and we are puzzled. We did not think it would be so easy. But it cannot matter, and we must hurry. We sink through the back of his neck, following the probe that seized the control centers of the brain.

Quickly we send microscopic feelers down through the nerve network, branching, branching, until they reach the ends of the extremities and dig down into the deepest, smallest organs of the body. We test out the network gently, and control is effective. Before we go any further, we must take precautions. Jerkily, unsteadily, we move the body into the shadows. Clumsily, we lay the body down beside the building. We relax it all over. The searchers will have to be almost upon us before they see.

Relaxed, the body is more accessible, and we are eager; we are hungry. Feelers reach out through the blood vessels, absorbing food as they go. When that circuit is completed, we are satiated. Our hunger is appeased. We feel a relaxation ourselves, a lowering of our awareness, and we must fight it. There is much to do; there is no time for relaxation.

Now we must take the last step. We hesitate, not knowing why we hesitate, and we send out a final set of feelers through the alien brain, searching for the seat of memory. We find it. We begin to learn. We learn more as we go deeper. We learn a new identity.

My name is Smith. George Smith. I am a laborer. I have a wife and four children. An identification card in my billfold describes a man, but it isn't me. Thirty years old, it says. Brown hair, brown eyes. Five feet nine. One hundred sixty pounds. Scar on right forehead. Tatoo of woman on left forearm. That isn't me. Figures lie. I am bigger than that; I am taller than that. I am only working as a laborer until something better comes along.

I've been picking up things that people left behind when they were ordered out of here. They call it looting, but it isn't that. It isn't stealing. Somebody else will take the things if I don't. The soldiers—don't tell me that they don't do all right by themselves when they go through those places. Besides, the things belong to me as much as anybody else . . .

It goes on and on, not like that, slow and ponderous, but as swiftly as thought spanning the galaxy until we know almost as much about Smith as he knows, and maybe more. We do not enjoy it. The unpleasantness of the man named Smith is only part of the price we must pay. But we hold back a little still, and it consoles us that we will leave him when his body has taken us to a place of safety and peace. But we will still have his memories. They will stay with us forever.

The automatic processes of the feelers have begun. Subtly the body is strengthened. Glands are stimulated. Tissues are regenerated. Wastes and old, accumulated poisons are removed. But basically we do not change anything. The man named Smith must remain physically the same and undetectable. It is irony that the body we have taken possession of is now almost immortal. It is vulnerable only to accidents. Our automatic responses will repel disease and revitalize aging tissues and perform innumerable other tasks which protoplasmic bodies can do poorly, if at all. The capabilities are there, but the inefficient brain does not use them. The body is immortal, and yet, when we leave, it must die.

Now, of all the possible hosts on Earth, this one has a director; it can enjoy the blessings of sanity and direction.

It has been a rape, not the meeting of two mutually acquiescent parts, incomplete in themselves, together a whole entity which is more than the sum of both. With our former host, it had been a pleasant, gently sensual experience of uniting and sharing, and afterwards it had been a completeness, a partnership by which both parties profited. Here there had been no chance of that. We knew it from the beginning. These things called men are too independent.

Now we have an identity. Survival dictates that we become that identity. We must act like it; a slip means destruction. We must think like it. We must be "we" no longer. We are one. We are I. I am a man named Smith.

I open my eyes and see. Lights are close. I see them shining, burning, only a block or two away. On the other side, too, they will be as close, or closer, and all around. Soon they will be here, and I must think quickly. For they will shoot this body, and I would have to leave again, and this time there would be no second chance.

There are things in my pockets that do not belong to me. If they are found on me, it will be disastrous. I take them out, rings, watches, money, and I drop them through the grating on which I lie. But there is one thing in the pockets I do not drop. It is a bottle. It is a small bottle; it fits in my hand, sloshing gently. I raise it to my lips with a gesture that is almost automatic, my nostrils wrinkling away from the sharp odor. I drink. I cringe from the body's reaction, and then I drink again and let some of the liquid dribble down my chin onto my clothes.

I listen. I hear a shot, not far away. Somebody screams and is silent.

The next moment a blinding light shines through my closed eyelids.

I make a loud, breathing noise, trying to hide my fear. I lie there, wondering if they will shoot or burn me with flames, and the moment is eternity.

"Oh, hell! It's only a drunk!"

"We oughta shoot him. That's our orders."

"Look at him. He musta been layin' there all night."

"I can't shoot him. Can you?"

"Let's take him to the Captain."

"Wake up, there! Wake up!"

Prodding. Eyes fluttering open, peering out, glazed and dull, into the light. One arm coming up across the eyes, protectively.

"Hey you! Get up!"

"Whassa matter? Whass goin' on?"

"Get up. Up on your feet!"

"Can't man lay down for a little snooze? Eh?"

"Come on! Get up! We ain't got all night."

"Aw right, aw right."

I wobble to my feet. I stand there swaying. I see their noses wrinkling, and I smell the sharp odor again. They close in upon me. They lead me off. I stumble along between them, my head drooping, for an interminable time.

"What's your name?"

"Name? Name's Smith. George Smith. What's yours?"

"Ugh! Search his pockets. Get out his identity card, too."

They fumble through my pockets and pull out my billfold. The world wants to spin around me. I let it spin.

"Occupation?"

"Eh?"

"What's your line of work?"

"Work for Rieger. Warehouse. Big man, Rieger. Lotsa money, lotsa 'nfluence. 'Ma union man. Citizen. Got my rights."

"What were you doing here?"

"Can't man lay down for little snooze? Eh? No law 'gainst it. Eh? Broke a law or somethin'? Pay fine? Okay." I reach fumblingly for my billfold. It is gone. I let my hand drop.

"Oh, hell! Let him go! Give him back his billfold, and one of you had better escort him through the lines. Get his head shot off otherwise."

A long, stumbling walk through darkness and sudden light, alternating, until suddenly there is nothing but darkness, and we stop.

"Okay, Bud. You're out. From here on, you're on your own. Just keep heading that way, and I hope you don't remember anything in the morning. Because if you do, you'll start shaking and you won't be able to stop."

I am shaking now, inside. I am weak as he disappears into the dark, and I don't know whether it is because I am unused to this alien body or because of the liquid I drank which my feelers have picked up from the veins. I reach out again. I reach out to contact the Enemy again, and it is more difficult now, because of the body or the liquid or the weak shaking, but I find him at last.

"It isn't over. The search can't be over. They haven't found it yet."

"They've met. The searching parties have come together. They've gone all over the public library, and there isn't any place else for them to search. Relax, Burke, the thing is dead."

"No, no, Ellis. It's alive, I tell you. They missed it somewhere. You haven't been on top of this thing like I have. While you've been getting your leg set, I've been directing this operation, and I've got a feeling for it. The monster is lurking somewhere. It isn't dead."

"You've been with it too long. You've been with it ever since we landed on that damned planet. Now it's hard for you to realize that it's over. Look at it logically. The soldiers went over that section of town with a tea strainer. They didn't miss a thing. You've done a good job, Burke. I'll see that you get credit for it."

"Damn it, I don't want credit. I want that thing dead. I want to see it for myself and know it's dead. I don't want to dream about it any more. If the troops got it, why didn't they report that they had?"

"How long do you think it would last in the inferno of a flame thrower? I saw them working as I came across town.

Whoosh! Whoosh! Firing at shadows. And that's how it would vanish. Just like a shadow. No one would know. It's incinerated now; there's nothing left."

"Yes, and maybe it's hiding somewhere. Some cranny that the soldiers missed. They aren't perfect. A crack in the pavement. A water pipe. A thousand places they wouldn't think of."

"And starved to death. It wasn't meant to live independently. It was a parasite, which means that it couldn't exist for very long without a host."

"Not necessarily. Some parasites have a free-living stage; others have one or more intermediate hosts. But analogies are useless and deceptive. This isn't one of our parasites. It's extraterrestrial, and it may not follow terrestrial patterns. Even granting that it would die within a few hours of free-living, that leaves one terrible possibility."

"What's that?"

"Maybe it found a host."

"An animal, you mean? A dog or a cat? Or a bird?"

"Or a man."

"But you ordered all the looters shot."

"I know, I know. But if only one escaped, through somebody's carelessness or somebody's misplaced softness. . . ."

It is folly to linger here in the darkness any longer. But I hesitate, and I catch one last thought.

"There's only one thing to do. Nobody leaves the city until we've checked on them. All animals are to be incinerated. We'll have to have the biggest manhunt and extermination this country has ever seen . . ."

I hurry away. I don't much care which way I go, and I walk purposelessly along the dark streets, spotted occasionally with overhanging lights. I can't leave the city. Not now, anyway. I will have to wait until their measures fail. They must fail, now, and their only chance is for me to make a slip. If I can act like all the rest of the hosts, I will be safe and they will finally give up.

Meanwhile the pressure to divide, submerged for the moment, will grow stronger and stronger inside me, inside this alien body. I will have to keep it for a while yet, and I hate every moment of it. It is a leaden weight I am forced to push along. It is stubborn and fleshy and stupid.

My feet turn at a lighted doorway, and I push myself inside a room before I can stop. I stand in the doorway, blinking, wondering why I have come in, and it is a strange thing to be wondering.

"George!" someone says.

It is a woman, a female. She throws a soft arm around my neck and drags me farther into the room. The lights fight unsuccessfully through a smoky haze. There are booths along the sides, and chairs and tables in the center, and a bar across the other end of the room.

"Where you been?" the woman asks.

I search through Smith's memory for a face and a name, and I find them. Dolores. "I been watching the soldiers, Dolores," I say.

It is important that I do not arouse suspicions. In the next few days questions will be asked. I would like to leave this place, but I do not dare. There was something about Dolores in the memories I could not force myself to search. I must wait a little until my leaving will go unnoticed.

"What they lookin' for, hey, George?"

"How do I know? I'm a mind reader or something?"

"I bet it's a bomb. Somebody planted a bomb, and they're lookin' for it. That's it, I bet."

"Maybe. They were shooting people."

"No kiddin'! Here, have a drink."

A glass is thrust into my hand. A head is leaned against my chest; tangled hair brushes irritatingly against my face.

"Phew! You already had a few."

"So what?"

She leads me to a booth and forces me down into it and slides in beside me, her thigh hot against mine. "You ain't drinkin', George," she complains loudly. She leans toward me. "What you get?" she whispers.

I reach into her mind, reluctantly, shuddering at the maelstrom of twisted thoughts and fears and hopes and passions. She and Smith had been intimate. Just tonight she persuaded

Smith to sneak into the closed area to pick up whatever he could find.

"Nothin'," I say.

"Nothin'!" She says it loudly, angrily. Quickly, she begins to whisper again. "What you mean by that? Why didn't you get anything? What are you trying to do, hold out on me?"

"Oh, shut up!"

"Maybe you think you can push me around," she says, her voice rising. "Maybe you think you can cheat me and get away with it. Think again. Remember, I can tell them you was in there. They wouldn't like that, I bet. I bet I could get you in a lot of trouble."

"For God's sake, shut up!" I whisper violently. "You'll get us both in trouble. Don't you understand? I couldn't get in. They were shooting people, anybody they saw, and then they were burning them. Maybe you'd rather I was laying in there, dead and fried."

She sags against the back of the booth; her body is a mass of fat curves with creases between them. "Oh, well, it was a chance. What we couldn't have done with a few thousand, eh, Georgie?" Her voice is wistful. "You could have skipped out on your wife and brats, and I could have skipped with you, and we could've ditched this town and had a gay old time. Oh, hell! Drink up, Georgie. Tomorrow we die."

I raise the glass and take a swallow and almost gag. I feel it burn down my throat and lay burning in the pit of my stomach. The rising fumes make my head swim. Her leg presses more firmly against mine as she leans over against me and puts her arms around me and lays her head on my shoulder.

"We still got our health, eh, Georgie?" she says. "We still got each other."

"Yeah," I say.

"Come on up to my room," she whispers. "We'll show the world what we care."

I catch a glimpse of her mind. It is wide open, and I am sickened. I try not to show it. I try to act reluctant.

"Can't," I say, and the words are difficult to get out as if the lips are trying to form another word. "Late now. I got to work tomorrow. And Agnes is gonna raise hell as it is."

She sits up sullenly. "Funny you never thought of any of that before."

The thing I want most in the world is to stop touching her. "I had a bad time tonight," I say. "A coupla times they almost caught me."

"Poor Georgie!" she says quickly, sympathetically. Her hand reaches out to stroke my face. "I didn't know it was gonna be that bad."

I try to stand up. The room wobbles. "I got to get out of here," I say. "I don't feel good."

"Sure, George. Finish your drink."

I hesitate, and the glass is halfway to my lips before I know it, and I let it come the rest of the way and drink it down. She slips out of the booth, and I slip out, and she stands next to me, hanging on my shoulder.

"Tomorrow night?" she whispers.

The body feels sick, and I feel sick inside the body. But it's worse than that. I'm afraid.

"Yeah," I get out through stiff lips, and I find my mouth brushing against hers, and I pull myself away. I thread my way between the tables, unsteadily, and I get out into the night, and I'm breathing deeply.

The next thing I know I'm climbing steep steps in a dark corridor, and I don't know how I got there.

I'm not climbing alone. Fear is climbing with me.

I climb and I turn and I climb again, and the darkness is thick with stale odors of cooked food. I try to figure out what I'm doing here and how I got here, but I feel vague and feeble, and the body, staggering a little, keeps climbing purposefully. Except that it can't have a purpose; I am its purpose. I can stop, if I want, but I let the body go on to its unknown destination.

I stop in front of a dark door. My hand reaches out. It has a key in it. The key fits into the keyhole and rattles and turns. The other hand eases the door open. I slip through into the room beyond and close the door gently behind me.

I walk through the room, maneuvering around unseen objects unerringly, although my feet are heavy and clumsy, and I find my hand on the knob of another door. I turn it gently.

It begins to open. It creaks. I hesitate.

"George?" It is a low, harsh voice, disembodied in the darkness.

"Yeah."

"So you finally came home."

There is no welcome here. The voice is bitter and spiteful.

I walk into the room and ease myself into a chair I don't know is there, and I reach out wearily toward the voice in the darkness. There is a bed there, and a woman is on the bed, and the woman is Smith's lawful mate. While I am Smith, she is my lawful mate. I touch her mind and recoil.

Hate! Violent and vicious. Hate doubled because it was once something else. Hate redoubled because it is impotent.

My hands reach down to untie my shoes. But inside the body, I am searching frantically for an excuse to get away. And I can't think of any.

"You run out of money or did Dolores get tired of you?"

"Nuts!" I say.

"You have something to eat?"

"Yeah."

"We had mush."

"Yeah."

"That's the third time this week."

"So what?"

"I'd think you'd want your kids to have a decent meal once in a while."

"I give you money," I say loudly. "It ain't my fault you throw it away on candy and magazines and movies."

"What else I got?" she says. "Fat lot of money you give me."

A distant voice says, "Mama!"

"You woke up the kids again," she says wearily.

I hear the bedsprings creak. A moment later an overhead light comes on. I blink. She is in a thin, ragged nightgown. Her face is haggard and old, but the body under the gown is still young. She walks by me, and I find my hand reaching out toward her. She twists away from it. She looks at me with hard, hating eyes, and her mouth curls with revulsion. She walks through the door and into the darkness beyond.

The bedroom is dirty and disheveled. The light glares down from a naked bulb hanging on a cord. It swings back and forth. Shadows sway around the room.

I reach out toward the other minds. They are young. They are overwise.

"He's home."

"I heard him. He's drunk again."

"Why does he have to come home? Why can't he stay away forever."

"Mama says we couldn't have nothing to eat."

"I don't care. I don't care if we eat mush all the time. It's better when he's gone."

"Sh-h-h. Mama's coming."

"Go back to sleep, boys. Everything's all right."

"He's home, ain't he, Mama?"

"Yes. Go back to sleep."

"Why can't he stay away?"

"Don't say things like that. He's your father."

"He ain't hurt you, has he, Mama?"

"No. Of course not."

"If he hurts you tonight, I'll kill him. I'll kill him."

"Me, too."

Hate. Pouring out at me. Surrounding me. Pressing down . . .

"You mustn't say things like that. He's your father."

"He's not! He's not!"

"Be quiet now. Go back to sleep."

She returns. I hear her footsteps echoing through the dark, the sticky, odorous dark, and I look around the room, and I wonder why I am here, so far from the clean meadows and the calm, gentle hosts of my home world. And I wonder how soon I can get away. I wonder if I must spend a night here, or more, sleeping in that bed beside the body of the woman, sensing her movements, listening to her thoughts, torn with repugnance. She is an enemy . . .

I have lived with danger for a long time. Ever since the ship descended upon our world, danger has walked beside me. It didn't matter so much there, because we were many, but now I am one and alone, and I am afraid.

These men are strange animals, and I, who have strange powers they never suspected until recently—I am afraid of them.

I am in the body of a man named Smith, and I hate it. *Smith! Smith! Where are you, Smith!*

The light is out and I crawl into bed beside the woman. I lie on one side of the bed, and she lies on the other, and we listen to each other breathing. I feel her hate.

I try to plan how I will get out of the city and how I will leave this alien body and seek the peace I need before I can divide. I think how I will find some of the animals that Smith heard of, and I will use them as hosts until I am many again, and we will take over this world. Once there are many of us, it will be simple. It will be painful work, but simple.

But it is useless. All I can think about is the woman lying there on the other side of this uncomfortable bed, and how I am surrounded by strange flesh and the flesh is surrounded by hate.

I am shocked to find myself in the middle of the bed. The discovery paralyzes me for a moment, and then I try to draw back. But there are odd, undefinable things working inside me. Uncontrolled sensations quiver along the nerves inside the body, quiver along the feelers that lie microscopically inside the nerves. Glands are discharging their secretions into the body. The process seems automatic; I can't stop them. The body, too, must have automatic responses. It reaches toward the woman.

"George!" she says in a low, vicious voice. "Get away from me."

I put my hand on her. She writhes away from it, her flesh shrinking. I get closer. She struggles; she hits at me with her fists. I pin her hands behind her with one of mine. I lower my head over hers, kissing her lips that twist like snakes under mine.

"George! Don't!" she snaps, when I raise my head for a moment. "The children are listening."

"So what?"

The body goes on doing things that I can't control. I can't

control anything now. Flesh speaks to flesh, and the emotions working inside me are wild and violent. I try to shut myself away from them. I try to cower back, to disengage myself, but it is no use.

"George," she says. I hear the voice distantly. "George! You filthy beast! Don't come crawling to me after you've been with that woman!"

But her voice is softening, and her body is softening, too. As I release her hands, they do not claw at me. They try to push me away, but they are weak and ineffectual.

Horror is inside the body with me, and I cannot help what the body is doing. Sweat rolls off our bodies.

"You beast," she says again. "You beast." But her voice is different now. She isn't pushing me away any more.

And the worst part is that beneath that surface response is the hate, still there, as violent and unappeasable as ever.

Later I find myself lying on the other side of the bed again. My senses are dulled with horror, and the body is dull, too. It is drifting into sleep.

"You devil," the woman says in a wild, torn voice. "I hate you."

And the body sleeps, soddenly.

But *I* do not sleep. I cannot sleep, like the body, and forget. I must lie awake and remember. And one thought, violent and powerful, drives all the others before it. *Escape!*

Get away, now! Get free from the body before it wakes again and does other terrible, uncontrollable things. There is danger! Ignore it! Pull free now, before it's too late.

I know that I can't stand it any longer. I must be free again. Perhaps this time I can find an animal, some pet, or better, a small animal like a rat. It will have holes and secret ways which the Enemy can't find. Unlike us, he has been unable to exterminate his pests. He will not be able to do it now.

The danger is great, but the danger of staying is greater. I try to begin the slow process of extricating myself from this fleshy trap. But the long, slender feelers will not slip from the nerves and the vessels. They are entangled, glued fast. Is that it? Or am I so weak that I can't even control my own extensions any longer?

The body holds me, clinging to every part of me. It won't let me go. I cannot move. I pull with all my strength. I send out imperious commands along the tenuous feelers. Nothing. Nothing happens.

There is only one chance left. I hesitate before taking it, but at last I send out the impulses of destruction and dissolution. I don't know what it will do to me, caught as I am inside this body, but I don't care any more. And it does nothing.

Trapped!

I relax, hopelessness and dismay washing over me like the ancient sea from which we came. I am caught, irretrievably, finally. I have no control over the body at all; I no longer have any control over my own being. Somehow, inexplicably, the powerful, instintive reactions of this monstrous body have welded me to it. We are bound together, indissolubly, until death.

A lifetime of terror and horror stretches before me. I am a consciousness imprisoned in a mass of flesh. Speechless, cut off from the world, I will live only to suffer.

Smith! Smith! Where are you?

But there is no answer. Smith is gone. It isn't Smith who has me, who will not let me go; it is this body. A lifetime!

There is one chance, one chance for freedom. There is one place I can turn for help. The Enemy can free me, and it no longer matters if the freedom is death.

I reach out once more, desperately.

Search! Search! Find him!

"Your plan is fantastic. I flatly refuse to let this city be shut down any longer."

"Gardner's right, Burke. You can take over a city for a few hours, but when you start talking about days it's impossible. And you can't expect any results."

"Okay, Ellis. The plan was foolish. I give up."

"Wait a minute. I'm all out of breath. I was all prepared to argue with you, and now you give up. You must have thought of something."

"I just started thinking of the thing as a parasite. Parasites are usually particular about their hosts. They're adapted to one species or a few closely allied species, and they can't change quickly. If the thing escaped, I imagine it found its host body uncongenial."

"Exactly, Burke. And I was going to make another point. In the struggle for existence, the parasite has chosen a negative reaction. It has followed the line of least resistance, giving up freedom and independence for protection and a more constant and usually richer supply of food. It's a retreat from struggle. Basically, it can't compete with positive reactions."

"Nevertheless, we must send out a ship immediately to wipe that world clean. We can't give them a chance to adapt."

"Just before I left the ship, I received new orders from Secspace."

"I suppose the thing is dead. . . ."

I slip away, my last hope gone. They will not search me out. *The monsters! The monsters!* The thing isn't dead, but it would like to be. It must live on until the host dies. . . .

Dies! I remember. With a horrible, sickened feeling, I remember. The rejuvenating network I have supplied this body has made it almost immortal.

My tormented imprisonment isn't just for a lifetime. It is forever.

The sodden body sleeps, this monster named Smith, while my thoughts race madly.

The body shivers, very gently. Deep inside it, a mute voice is screaming.

3. Cinderella Story

ALYN WAS A XENOLOGIST. She was also a woman. The xenologist was worried. The woman was scared. The natives were throwing a ball, and she had a horrid suspicion that her teammates would insist she go.

She slipped through the market place, unnoticed in the blaze of noon, and damned private enterprise. . . .

Private enterprise made ET exploration possible. Government could do it, but Government wouldn't. That had been proved. Space was fantastically big, and ET exploration was fantastically expensive. ET exploration was also vital: humanity needed a frontier for the good of its soul; for the good of its body it needed that frontier as far as possible from Earth.

Laws were drafted to make exploration profitable, and humanity was unleashed upon the galaxy, *Jonathan Craddock, Exploiters and Importers*, was born—along with one hundred competitors, more or less.

The Bureau of Extraterrestrial Affairs was born at the same time to enforce the laws and regulate the profit.

If an exploration team located an uninhabited world or a Level 6 culture—stringently defined by BETA regulations as one ready for terrestrial contact—the company received an exclusive franchise to exploit that world. In actual practice only the Level 6 discovery was worthwhile. Exploitation of an inhabited world was theoretically possible, but at this stage of Earth's technological development, the capital outlay was prohibitive. A company could wait five years for a profit; it couldn't wait a hundred.

On the other hand, one Level 6 discovery recouped a thousand failures. Virgin trade territory was fabulously profitable.

Exploration teams had two assets: the Fairfax field, that subtle electronic gadget which persuades those creatures within its range that they see what they are expecting to see; and the quality of their members, who were motivated by that most reliable of incentives—greed. Their rewards were graduated sharply according to achievements up to a Level 6 plateau which made each team member independently wealthy for life.

Labor unions objected to the incentive system; idealists objected to the motives. Both worked. The persons who signed company contracts sought not security but adventure, not ends but means. They were neither morally better nor worse than the ordinary run of humanity, but they were more determined, more persistent, more ingenious, and more trustworthy.

The teams had an equal number of debits: since the companies could not wait centuries, the teams had to move fast; and speed means mistakes through lack of understanding. Like idioms. The Translators were good, but only experience can translate idioms. . . .

That thought bothered Alyn most as she threaded her way through the crowded street back toward the ship. A native turned sharply and looked at her with surprised violet eyes. Then she drew closer, and his eyes went blank. Alyn shivered, although Meissner's Star was hot, and drew her cloak closer around her.

"When there's dirty work to be done," she thought rebelliously, "I'm the one who has to do it."

Her lips moving silently, she damned them: Davis, Pip, and the Skipper—her teammates, her men, her children, her lovers. . . . Long ago Earth's voyagers had found the ideal spaceship complement: three men and a woman. Carefully selected, a woman could easily be all things to three men, and three men, if they tried hard, could be all things to a woman.

But they imposed on her, as men do upon a woman who loves them. They expected her to slave for them all night and all day, too, while they lolled at home. . . .

She focused her desires on reaching the spaceship that towered tall and iridescent in the distance. Home. They would be waiting for her. Her face softened, grew feminine and lovely. Quiet, loyal Davis—the methodical scientist, at home with things, asea in human relations, never expecting anything, always grateful for whatever he received. Little, effervescent Pip—the sure-fingered technician, shrewd, impertinent, and easily hurt. The Skipper—big, blond, self-sufficient, monosyllabic, avuncula . . . .

He was older than the others, Alyn thought, but not that old. She would have to be particularly attractive to him—

A native jostled her back to awareness. She almost screamed. Panicky, she clutched the cloak, hugged it tight. The Fairfax Field was a wonderful thing—it made xenological field work possible—but it was less deceptive in daylight. At the periphery, the natives were catching glimpses of her as she really was. Soon they would start putting the extraordinary together, and they would get "alien."

Then, at best, the Team would be out—with the Company on its back and the Bureau on its neck.

While she was about it, she damned the Company, too. It cut a corner, saved a penny, and lost a world. These Field generators were obsolescent, and she was getting a bounce effect that made her observations virtually worthless. It was all very well for the natives to see her as a native and the Ship as a native dwelling, but when she saw their world as vaguely Earthlike, the whole enterprise became pointless. It was impossible to tell what was real and what was Fairfax. . . .

The town was an eighteenth century English village trembling perilously on the brink of the Industrial Revolution . . . but not quite.

The picture was just a little askew, as if the signboard of the village inn illustrated a beheading with half a dozen natives lying, mouths open, to catch the blood as it fell.

As a matter of fact, that *was* the signboard of the village inn. It was, apparently, an idiom—or, at least, the way in which Alyn's mind, reinforced by the bounce effect of the Fairfax Field, interpreted the native idiom. Probably it was not that at all.

So it went. The houses were not quite the proper shape. They were built solidly enough of bricks or stone, but they were painted with intricate, painstaking, many-colored designs.

She came out of the market place into the green common. She threaded her way between grazing ruminants that were not quite cows and restrained an impulse to run. She walked down a street that was not quite cobblestone among creatures that were not quite human.

They were man-shaped, but their torsos were too long and oddly distorted, pigeon-breasted, as if there were too many bones inside. Their arms were short, and their hands had only four fingers, like cartoon characters. Their heads were small and their faces malformed, with pushed-in noses, large, bulging violet eyes, wide mouths and pointed teeth, and prognathous jaws.

They looked like hairless Pekingese dogs, a caricature of humanity that made Alyn want to scream.

Their name for themselves translated as "the People." The Team called them "Pekes," against all rules—BETA, Company, and scientific. By extension, Meissner's Star (2) became "Peking."

The Pekes made Alyn nervous. She didn't mind creatures that scampered or writhed or swam or oozed, but she couldn't stand creatures who walked on two legs and looked her in the eye. If they weren't human, they gave her the willies.

They were humanoid—the Fairfax Field couldn't falsify that. And that was just what made any conclusions dangerous.

Alyn scrambled up the ladder. The spaceship door swung open. She walked through the air lock, went through the inner door, and climbed the stairway to the living deck.

Davis turned from his workbench, a test tube forgotten in his fingers. Pip looked up from the delicately carved lapis lazuli he was examining through a loupe. The Skipper swung down from the bridge. They looked at her expectantly, a little greedily.

Alyn said, "They're going to have a ball."

She let the cloak and hood slip down. It crumpled on the

floor. Underneath it she was wearing a halter and shorts. She had a good figure—slim and youthful, but womanly.

She had the type of face that is best described as fascinating. Partly it was her red hair, but it was more the face: forehead too high, cheekbones too prominent, lips too firm, chin too stubborn, eyes too intelligent. They made a combination men found irresistible, but she was too sane to make it her fortune.

Perhaps that was why she had joined *Jonathan Craddock*. Or maybe it was the money. Nowhere else could a woman retire at thirty, unencumbered, with enough money to let her do what she wished for the rest of her life—if her team were lucky enough to hit upon that one-in-a-hundred Level 6 culture.

Or maybe it was because only with *Jonathan Craddock*—or a competitor—could she practice legalized polyandry. Had she, as woman always had, followed the interesting men, the voyagers, the risk-takers? It was a question she had been unable to answer for herself. She knew only that the ones left at home were culls.

"Careful with that cloak," Davis said absently. "There's ten thousand bucks' worth of Fairfax Field wired into that rag."

Alyn scowled at him. "And it doesn't work. I'm getting too much bounce effect." She shrugged and turned away. "No matter, anyhow. No more daylight work for me. It's too hot in that cloak, and too dangerous."

Pip chuckled. "Trust the incredulity factor, Alyn."

"Don't blabber."

But Pip was probably right. That was how the Field worked. Or how it was thought to work; there was a lot of disagreement. Fairfax himself had always insisted that it did no more than satisfy the brain's visual scanning mechanism, the alpha rhythm; it stopped—or interfered with—the scanning sweep, giving the watcher the sense of seeing something without specifying what that something was. From there on, the incredulity factor took over—that habit of the mind which directs it to seek always the simpler explanation. That there are aliens among us is a wild fantasy; it is simpler to assume that what one sees is something ordinary, seen badly.

But not every mind has an alpha rhythm to interrupt—for instance, M-types. Some epistomologists doubted that the Field affected the mind at all, and photographs supported them: an object inside a Fairfax Field *was* optically blurred, even to the mindless eye of a camera. But if that were all there was to it, why the bounce effect—and the critical tuning that made it possible to get rid of it?

"I don't think it's just the incredulity factor," Alyn said slowly. "The Pekes are just humanoid enough to make us forget that they're aliens. But *we're* the aliens; *we* don't expect to see something ordinary here, unless the Field is leaking. And I think it is. It rattles me, Pip."

"The ball," the Skipper prompted.

Alyn started. "That's what the Translator called it. A dance with music. If they dance and if they have music. Maybe it's a party where they play footsie and later pay the piper. Who can be sure with an idiom?"

"Who's throwing it?" Davis asked.

"The king, chief, elder, headman—whatever you want to call him. If he's any of those. We can't overestimate our inability to translate accurately."

"Understood," the Skipper said impatiently.

"Well," Alyn continued reluctantly, "he lives in that big pile of masonry on the hill above town. He's got a male offspring—or maybe it's an heir-designate from the village—anyway, he's come of age, and the king has invited all the nubile maidens in the kingdom to a ball at which the prince will take his pick. For what purpose I can only guess. It isn't even safe to guess. . . ." She looked at the Skipper and read something in his eyes which made her look quickly at Pip and even quicker at Davis. "No," she said weakly, and then more defiantly, "No! NO! I won't do it. You can't make me do it!"

"Big chance," the Skipper pointed out. "Ceremony. Good evidence."

"You're the woman," Pip said, "and the xenologist."

"It's now or never," Davis added.

"Then it's never," Alyn said breathlessly. "Mixing with Pekes at an affair like that! Anything might happen. My cloak could be pulled away. . . ."

Pip reassured her. "I'll take care of that."

"Let's give up on Peking. We're wasting our time. It'll never pay out. The Pekes aren't Level 6 or even Level 5. Anyway, they've got nothing worth exporting."

"Maybe," the Skipper said, shrugging. "Still a chance."

"There's the jewels and the engravings," Davis said.

"Al's right," Pip said. "We can't collect enough secretly to make it worthwhile. Extra-T curios are scarcely worth hold space, anyhow. But Level 6! You never can tell about the Bureau. Tell the truth, Al. Why don't you want to go to the ball?"

She burst into tears of weariness and frustration. "Because I've got nothing to wear, stupid!"

"Is that all?" Pip said slyly.

"Last chance," the Skipper said bluntly.

Alyn snapped, "Well, why don't one of you go?"

"Oho!" Pip chortled. "The Field is good, but not good enough to turn us into nubile maidens. It will have to work hard enough on you."

"You're hateful!" Alyn snapped, stamping her foot. "When we get back, one of us can just find another group, that's all!"

"She'll go," said the Skipper.

Alyn came out of her cabin with a swish and a swirl of musical white crinoline that made three masculine jaws drop in admiration. She was a creature of elegance and radiant beauty, from her transparent shoes to her living crown of coiled hair sparkling with tiny stars. She was every man's desire. . . .

Pip recovered first. "You've got the Field turned on!"

"Say, now," Davis protested. "We've got to live with you, you know. That's not fair."

"Right," the Skipper said.

Alyn pivoted on her right heel and faded. Not much. Just enough to appear only humanly desirable. "Serves you right. You're mean, sadistic beasts, all of you, and I don't know why I ever signed on." She looked down at her dress, spun slowly around, and couldn't sustain a frown. She sighed. "It's beautiful."

For once all of them were silent. Finally Davis said, "We wanted to give you a present."

Pip added softly, "We saved it for a moment when you needed it most."

"Surprise," said the Skipper.

Alyn's frown returned. "And you gave it to me now so that I'd do your dirty work for you. Men!" She turned sharply on Pip. "The reason I turned on the Field—I had to try it out. And I got a frightful bounce effect."

Pip grinned. "We looked good to you, too, huh? Well, it figures. A small unit like that one in the heel of your right shoe can't carry much shielding. It's not centrally located either. A marvelous piece of micro-machining, though. Worth its weight in tickets home. One thing—the battery is good for only four hours. Be back before then."

"It's battery-operated?" Alyn exclaimed.

"Just the receiver. The Field itself is picked up from the ship. Don't worry—as long as you get back within four hours."

"Fine, wonderful," Alyn muttered. "Eight-nine-ten-eleven-twelve. Pip isn't this a little thick? Who do you think you're fooling with this fairy tale?"

Pip looked sheepish. "It's a gamble."

"You lost. I won't go."

Davis protested, "But there's no time to change our plans."

"Right," said the Skipper. "Pip's sorry. No difference. Must go."

"Fairy tale themes are endlessly repetitive," Pip said. "The good ones, anyway. That's why they persist. They express something fundamental about existence." After a moment he added: "We'll be there too, you know."

Alyn's face softened. "I might have known you wouldn't toss me out completely on my own. Who's going to carry the camera?"

"I—" Davis began, and stopped.

Alyn took a deep breath. "Okay. Don't drop it. I don't know where I'm going, but I'll want to know where I've been

—and who I was at the time."

She made her way down the treads to the air lock and through it and down the ladder to the ground as carefully as a conductor threading his way through an orchestra pit. The dress was an encumbrance, but it was also a necessity. She would have been better off in a cloak, but she would never have gone in a cloak.

Behind her came Davis and Pip. To her they looked like Davis and Pip in hood and cloak. To Pekes they would look like Pekes—perhaps. That was the beauty of the Fairfax Field: it reinforced the expected image.

Or did it? Suppose the Pekes were M types, *Minus* the alpha rhythm, wholly visual thinkers whose minds were so busy manipulating images that they had no scanning pattern to interrupt? Or suppose they were P-for-Persistent types, wholly abstract thinkers, whose alpha rhythm went on constantly without their feeling any need to satisfy it? Fairfax had been wrong, he had to be wrong. The field, had he been right, should work only for R-for-Responsive types, whose visual scanning stopped when they actually saw something, or their brains threw up a visual thought that substituted for an actual sighting. That would explain the disagreement on how it worked, for human beings were a mixed lot—mostly R.

If the Pekes were a mixed lot too, that left only the incredulity factor—quite unreinforced, except by the optical effect of the Field. It was not much to lean on.

She walked along the streets that were not quite cobblestone streets in her dancing slippers, one heel of which contained a Fairfax Field receiver and amplifier. The street was immaculate. That was one point for the Pekes—they were clean, unlike the pseudo-England she was seeing through the Field. . . . She stopped herself. Comparisons of that kind were the xenologist's pitfall; the use of the Field prohibited them. Too much bounce effect.

Just once she looked back at the ship. To her it looked like a ship—a wonderful shiny fortress of a ship, but still a ship. To the Pekes—perhaps—it looked like a native fortress that had been there ever since they could remember.

Providing the Pekes were all R's—*and* providing that the

Field had anything at all to do with the alpha rhythm.

There was scarcely anyone on the street: a few late shoppers hurrying home, a policeman sauntering along, checking the stores. . . .

A policeman!

He saw Alyn and smiled. "Ah, there," he said in a rich Irish brogue, "anither maiden for the ball, is it? You'd better be hurrying, me dear, or the Prince will have made his pick and you not there."

Alyn shivered. She was getting a bounce effect to end all bounce effects. A policeman, indeed! She bent her head and moved rapidly toward the large building on the hill.

As she drew near, it looked more like a palace than the native structure she remembered. She climbed the gleaming marble stairs and passed between tall columns to the big, brass doors. They swung open. A uniformed majordomo bowed her into a long hallway carpeted in red velvet. Its walls were hung with tapestries. . . . Tapestries!

She turned to run away, panic fluttering like a bird in her throat. But she glimpsed Davis and Pip skulking behind. They wouldn't let her quit. What they had, the Team, was based on confidence. Once it was shattered, the Team was broken, no good, and what they had was no good either. . . .

She turned back to the hallway.

It led her into a magnificent ballroom, its dark, parquet floor glistening in the light of dozens of candelabra hanging from the vaulted ceiling. The floor was crowded with beautiful women and handsome men, all dressed to the teeth, bejeweled and bespangled. They danced to the music of an orchestra that played on a distant platform.

As she hesitated, the dancers stopped. The music died away. Everyone's eyes turned toward her. Panic surged into her throat again. She bit her lower lip to keep from screaming.

Out of the throng came a man moving slowly, his dark eyes fixed upon her face. He was a tall man, broad-shouldered and lean, his face ruggedly handsome, his mouth betraying an unsuspected sensitivity. He wore a Graustarkian uniform, sparkling with buttons, jingling with medals. . . .

He was—the dream prince, the fairy tale prince, the answer to every maiden's prayer. . . . And he was just as real.

Still, Alyn could not resist a shiver of anticipation as he approached her. His eyes searched her face until he was very close; her knees got a little weak. His hand reached out for hers. He bowed low over it. His lips kissed her palm. For a frantic moment she thought of the Pekes' needle-sharp teeth. . . .

Her last really sane thought was: *How does this look to Davis and Pip . . .? What is really happening?*

Then she surrendered herself to the illusions of the Fairfax Field and the arms of the Prince.

The ballroom floor was like an undersea fairyland of color and music through which she swam like an infinitely graceful angelfish around which the Prince pirouetted and returned in a hypnotic mating dance. Around her moved other dancers. Music played distantly, something familiar although she could not quite place it. But neither one made any real impression upon her.

She had no eyes for anyone but the Prince, no ears for anything but his whispers. What did he say? Nothing and everything—she could not remember, and yet it was what should have been said, what had to be said. . . . She knew that at the time. Nothing was done to break the spell—for it was a spell; she knew it, and she could not change it, and she would not have changed it if she could.

She was falling in love. She was falling in love with a Peke, with a creature impossibly alien. She knew it and it didn't matter.

This was not like the love she felt for Davis and Pip and the Skipper. That had been an emotion slow in developing, even slower in being recognized for what it was: an emotion compounded of the maternal, the protective, the tolerant, and the sexual.

This was a love of another color. This was romantic love, a scarlet thing. The Prince was perfection; his touch made her faint. Life was bliss that would never end, a fire that raced through her veins, a tide that choked her throat, a delicious ache that turned her limbs languorous. . . .

She was in love with a dream, with a Field-induced delusion, but now it didn't matter. The emotion alone was enough.

Time passed like a blurred watercolor. She was delirious, feverish, enraptured, abandoned, reckless. . . . The Prince led her toward a small doorway, his hand holding hers, his eyes fixed upon her face. She followed dreamily. Wherever her Prince led, she would follow. His dear face preceded her, the cute, little upturned nose, the violet eyes, the wide, sensitive mouth. . . .

"Alyn!"

Someone was calling her. Who? No matter. Nothing mattered but the Prince.

"Alyn! Alyn! Alyn! Alyn! . . ." It went on like that, like the tolling of a bell. She couldn't ignore it; somehow she would have to silence it.

Her eyes cleared a little. Out of the surrounding blur came a face she knew. It was Pip's face. It was contorted, the mouth open, yelling at her. . . .

"Alyn! For crimeny's sake, the battery's failing. You're coming through. We've got to get out of here. What's the matter with you? Snap out of it! Alyn!"

The mists thinned. Her eyes swept the faces around her: Peke faces. Even the Prince's face was a Peke's face, beloved though it was. . . .

Sanity returned like a cold sea wave engulfing her. She would have to run. She turned wildly and fled through the hall. No longer was it a ballroom. It was a big, rough masonry meeting room filled with Pekes. The candelabra were open gas flames.

The Pekes gaped at her. They couldn't be seeing her clearly yet. But they could see that she was acting strangely. Soon they would try to stop her.

Behind her a Peke voice called out. The Prince. She knew it instinctively. Her heart turned over, but still she ran.

She reached the doorway. The tapestries were really the intricate Peke designs drawn upon the walls. The red velvet carpet was a rush mat. Her shoe caught in it. She almost fell, but her foot pulled free, and she ran on.

At the big front door the Peke guard looked at her with startled eyes, but he wasn't quick enough to catch her. She was through the rough, board doorway and into the pebbled street, racing through the night toward the ship. . . .

Halfway there, Pip caught up. He threw his cloak around her, and they ran together, side by side.

"Pip!" she sobbed gratefully. "Oh, Pip! What happened, Pip?"

"That's what I was going to ask you. That Peke waltzed up to you like you were his one true love, and you went into those damn arms of his like you knew it. He started stamping around you, and you stood there, turning slowly to face him, smiling. . . . Gosh, we were scared!"

"Where's Davis?" Alyn asked in sudden alarm.

"He wanted to film the Pekes' reaction to your flight," Pip said quickly.

"You mean," Alyn said, panting, "he was going to head them off if they got too close. You're wonderful, you and Davis. I couldn't have better teammates." *Teammates, team mates. . . . But what about her soul mate? What about the Prince?*

She hadn't answered Pip's questions, but then he hadn't asked any. Not directly. They were there, close to his lips, and she couldn't answer them. What she had been through was too real, too emotionally meaningful. She was still shaken.

Suddenly she said, "Pip! I lost my shoe!"

"Which shoe?"

"The right shoe. The one with the unit in it!"

Pip pulled them to a stop. "We've got to get it back!"

But the hill was black with Pekes swarming after them like bees out of a disturbed hive. Pip muttered, "Maybe Davis picked it up." And they ran again.

Eventually, long after Alyn had decided it would be easier to let the Pekes catch her than to draw another tortured breath, they reached the ship. They scrambled into it, and they waited.

For hours the Pekes milled through the streets, searching for the impossible creatures who had impossibly disappeared. After they gave up, Alyn, Pip, and the Skipper waited for

Davis. And waited, not talking. And waited, afraid to hope.
Just before dawn, he walked in, unruffled. They met him at
the air lock.

"Wow!" Davis said as he slipped out of his cloak and carefully hung it up. "They were ready to bite each other's heads
off. Did, as a matter of fact. The Prince acted like someone
had hit him in the head with an axe."

Alyn watched his face intently, her green eyes unreadable.
Impatiently, Pip said, "Did you get the shoe?"

"What shoe?" Davis asked blankly.

They sat around the living deck, three men and a woman,
waiting for something to happen. Pip fiddled with a micro-
mechanism, doing more damage than good. Davis pretended
to be interested in some tests he was running on an ore sample, but his gaze kept drifting toward the window. The Skipper
leaned back in his favorite chair, his hands thrust deep into
his pockets, not talking at all. Alyn sat in the window seat,
staring at the street below.

"What I can't understand," Davis said suddenly, not looking at Alyn, "is why she was going into that room with that
Peke."

"That's why I was there," Alyn said absently; "to find out
everything I could."

"We didn't really intend for that to cover the possibility of
cross-breeding," Pip said slyly. "Logically, this should be
reported to the Bureau of Extraterrestrial Affairs."

"Don't be ridiculous," Alyn said, but her heart wasn't in it.

"You knew, of course," Pip went on, his eyes studying Alyn
intently, "that it was a symbolic marriage. After consumma-
tion, the bride is sacrificed as the repository of the bride-
groom's youthful sins. He heads into manhood with a clean
slate."

"What I can't understand," Davis said plaintively, "is how
you expected to get out of that room."

"Maybe she didn't want to get out," Pip said slowly. "And
now the Prince is searching for her throughout the land."

Alyn turned sharply on Pip. "What's that?"

"He's got that shoe of yours. He's sent it around to all the workmen in the village to see if they made it." Pip got up and walked to the window. He stared out. "He's trying to find you, Al."

Alyn's green eyes searched Pip's face.

"Let's get out of here!" Davis exploded. "We've fouled this one up completely."

"No!" Alyn said.

"Why?" said the Skipper.

Alyn said flatly, "I changed my mind."

"Can't anyway," said the Skipper. "Bureau would quarantine Peking. Bar Company for good. Company'd fire us. No good. Two chances: Pekes Level 6 or get back shoe."

Pip said to Alyn, "Good thinking!"

"Shut up!" Alyn snapped.

"What's the matter with everybody?" Davis asked in bewilderment. "Nobody's been himself since the ball. Alyn"— he flushed—"hasn't been friendly. Pip has been picking on her. The Skipper hasn't said a word. What's the matter?"

Nobody answered him. Pip shrugged, stared out the window, and began whistling *After the Ball Is Over*.

"We're waiting for the end of the story," Alyn said.

"And here he comes now," Pip said.

"Where?" Alyn said harshly.

Pip pointed. "See where he comes with the shoe in his hand?"

The Peke marched steadily, purposefully toward the ship.

"Get this on film!" the Skipper snapped.

Davis sprang to the control room ladder.

The Peke got closer, became foreshortened, and passed beneath the curve of the ship. They waited, breathless. Davis backed down the ladder. They whirled on him and then turned back to their vigil.

The slow rasp of wood against metal drifted up to them. The Peke was climbing the ladder. The ship vibrated. Something rapped against the air lock door.

"Well?" Pip said.

Impassively, the Skipper said, "Let it in."

A little, involuntary wail broke from Alyn's lips. "I can't." She turned blindly and ran to her room. "Pip," she called back over her shoulder, "lock the door on that side."

She slammed the door behind her, slid the bolt across, and waited, her hand on it, until she heard the bolt outside click shut. It echoed in the little room with a grim finality. She threw herself onto her bunk and bit the pillow to keep from screaming.

Distantly she heard the air lock open below and then the slow clomp of feet on stair treads. Voices rumbled for a long time. Once she found herself at the door, her hand on the bolt, before she remembered that it was bolted on the other side, too.

She threw herself back onto the bunk.

Time dripped slowly in discreet seconds. Hours later the ship vibrated again. This time the feet were descending. The air lock opened and closed and feet went down the ladder outside. Someone pounded at the door.

"Alyn!" Davis shouted. "We've got it. The Skipper swears it will stand up in every court in the galaxy. It's Level 6."

Slowly, wearily, Alyn got up and went to the door. When she opened it, Davis was there, his face flushed and triumphant. He caught her around the waist, lifted her, swung her around, shouting, "Let's celebrate. We're rich, we're rich!"

Finally he lowered her to the floor. Alyn said, "What happened?"

Pip said, "He figured it out. The Prince. The reports came back to him: none of the village workmen had made that unit in the slipper. None of them had ever seen anything like it. They could duplicate it, but they couldn't have invented it. Q.E.D.—aliens.

"He had the whole village questioned, the results tabulated and compared, the discrepancies noted. Then he came here."

"Alone?" Alyn asked. "Unarmed?"

Davis said happily, "He wants more gadgets like that one. They do magic. He's ready to trade."

"What has he got to trade?" Alyn asked sharply.

Pip said, "Skill. Peking is a mine of micro-skills waiting to be refined. They've been developing them for centuries with that intricate design work. All the Pekes need is a few simple tools and they can duplicate any micro-mechanism. They're quick, smart, accurate. I told you that Fairfax Field micro-unit was worth its weight in tickets home—well, his workmen had made *ten* of them already."

"But the Pekes aren't Level 6," Alyn objected.

"If deducing our presence from the shoe and locating us through comparative interviews isn't Level 6," Davis said, "there isn't a CQ test worth the computer it's figured in."

The Skipper rumbled, "Proof, too. On film. Rich. All of us."

Alyn bit her full lower lip. "What—did he say—about me?"

Slowly, watching her face, Pip shook his head. "He didn't mention you. But he left this." He tossed Alyn the slipper.

She caught it without thinking and then turned it over slowly to look at it from all sides.

"The foot the shoe fitted," Pip said gently, "was his." Pip's eyes were unusually quiet and dark.

Alyn nodded gravely and turned slowly back toward her cabin.

Davis stopped smiling. "What's the matter with her?"

Pip shook his head impatiently.

"What I can't understand," Davis whispered, "is why she wanted her door locked from this side when the Peke was here."

Pip said softly, "She wasn't afraid the Peke was coming after her. She knew he was. She was afraid he would ask her to go with him, and she wouldn't be able to refuse."

"Go with a Peke!" Davis exclaimed.

"With a Prince," Pip said.

Alyn hesitated at the door. "Let's get out of here!" she said harshly. "We got what we came after. Let's get back to Earth."

Pip said, "And so they lived happily ever after."

Cinderella cried half the long way home.

4. *Teddy Bass*

I TOOK THE LAST STEP, and my foot sank into something soft. I pulled back and felt foolish. I knew what it was.

Lying on the cement of the porch, his sliding black pupils intent in their plastic corneas as he tried to understand the stars, was Brownie—Kit's teddy bear.

There's always something where it shouldn't be: a toy car, a round block, a tricycle. . . . That's kids. You try to tell them, and they say, "But I didn't leave it there, Daddy," and you'd like to believe them but you can't. Either they're lying, or there's an innate perversity in *things* that sneaks them into the way of the careless foot or the carefree shin, that wants us lame or dead. . . .

And you can't believe that, not unless you're crazy.

I picked up Brownie. He dripped.

I let it trickle onto my hand. Sawdust. I turned him over. Excelsior bulged through a slit in his abdomen.

I felt a little sick, seeing some childish hand slashing Brownie in a fit of anger. Or, worse, cold malice.

Please, I thought, *not Kit. Don't let it be Kit.*

I was trying to shove the excelsior back into the teddy bear when I remembered. The afternoon's scene returned to me as vividly and real as when I had seen it. Had I forgotten?

No one who had seen it would ever forget. The accident had been bad enough: the screaming of tires like living things and the brief, mechanical scream of the woman, cut off sharply, finally. But that wasn't the worst.

The worst was rushing to help and standing there helpless, seeing the woman's body on the street looking just like Brownie with the stuffing coming out, much cleaner and neater than anyone would expect and infinitely more horrible. Sawdust and excelsior.

Everything came back, the numbed feeling when my mind refused to work and the man next to me saying, with grisly, unconscious humor, "Well, it sure knocked the stuffing out of her."

And then the cold thoughts: *Some of us aren't real.* And: *Somebody slipped.*

But that was a foolish thought. I wasn't prepared to accept the inevitable consequences. It meant—

"Mr. Gunn?"

I swung around. There hadn't been any footsteps—at least, I hadn't heard any—but a man was behind me. He was dressed in a blue uniform with bright buttons. The light shining through the old-fashioned front door gleamed on the buttons and flashed from the badge on his chest. Policeman.

"Yes?" A police car was behind mine at the curb. A few seconds ago it hadn't been there.

"Come with me." He looked down at me, strength clothed in authority, his face impassive.

"Where?"

"To the station. You're wanted as a witness."

"To what?"

"To that accident you saw this afternoon. If you'll come with me, Mr. Gunn, we'll get this over in a hurry. All we want is a statement—"

"I don't want to go with you," I said, trying to make it firm, but, to my horror, my voice was high-pitched and squeaky like a child refusing to go to the dentist. Inside me a chant of terror was growing: *How did they know my name? Nobody took down my name. How did they find me?*

There probably was a simple explanation, but I couldn't think of it. And I couldn't ask because that would be admitting I had been there. Suddenly I was afraid to do that.

"You ain't got any choice, sir," the officer said.

"You can't just walk up to a man—practically in his home —and haul him off without a warrant or anything. . . ."

"The only one who tells me what I can't do is the Chief," the officer said politely. "Come along now."

"I don't know what you're talking about. I didn't see any accident."

"Oh, yes, you did, Mr. Gunn," the officer said positively. "We've got your name down on our list." He shook his head unhappily. "You not only saw it, you remember it. Somebody sure slipped on this one."

Turning incredulously, I

(   )

was sitting on a hard jail cot. The scene had shifted; there was no other way to describe it. One instant I was standing on my porch talking to the policeman; the next I was in a dark cell.

There were no memories for between.

My head didn't hurt, but I raised my left hand to it anyway. There were no lumps. Brownie was in my right hand. I stared down at the teddy bear, blankly, trying to remember.

Some new gas, I thought. *Odorless. Non-toxic.*

Only—why was I in jail?

"You not only saw it," the policeman had said, "you remember it. Somebody sure slipped on this one."

He'd been talking about the accident. Of course I remembered it. Why shouldn't I remember it? It happened, didn't it? I saw it, didn't I?

Suddenly, sitting there, I wasn't so sure. What had happened was more the texture of nightmare than reality. Nobody is stuffed, not with sawdust and excelsior or kapok or . . . And if I had seen an accident like that, I wouldn't have forgotten—not ever.

It was a dream—the accident, the policeman. . . . It had to be.

This, too?

Brownie felt real enough, his fur crisp against my hand, the sawdust trickling out of him gritty between my fingers. I pulled out my handkerchief and tied it around Brownie like a sash to keep him from sifting away before I got him home.

Home? I thought suddenly. Why wasn't I home? Why was I accepting this as reality? Surely I was home and this was all a dream.

The framework on the cot was hard and cold under my hand.

I crossed to the cell door and called out, "Jailor!" No answer. "Jailor!" I rattled the metal bars. "JAILOR!"

He came at last, a tall, lean, gloomy man in blue. "Whatsa matter?" he growled.

"I want out of here!"

"They all do."

"I've got no business being in here—"

"Nobody has."

"Somebody's made a mistake," I insisted. "I was supposed to come down to the station as a witness to a traffic accident. The next thing I knew I was in this cell."

"No use trying to pull this stuff on me, Gunn. I won't testify for you. What you need is an alienist. Wait for the trial."

"What trial?" I demanded.

"Your trial, Gunn. If you're lucky, you might get off with manslaughter."

He turned his back and moved away, chuckling. I sank back weakly on the cot. Manslaughter? Had I killed somebody? The policeman? Of course not. An armed man, as big and experienced as he was? And I hadn't the least memory—

That was the catch. No memory. People black out. Madness overwhelms their sanity, swamps their memories of violence. . . . Could I have killed someone?

I sat stonily on the cot, silent, probing. What does madness feel like? What are the symptoms? I couldn't find any signs— except the memories I had and the ones I lacked—but I wouldn't be a trustworthy judge if I were mad.

How does a man act it he thinks he might be mad? If he acts on the presumption he is insane, then he wouldn't be, would he?

But then every madman comes to this conclusion: If I am mad, it doesn't matter how I act; but if I am sane, I would be crazy to act as if I were mad.

It was identical with the dream-reality question. I must act as if I were awake and sane.

I picked up Brownie and wondered what day it was. Where were Kit and Jane; what were they doing? Did they know what had happened to me, or did they think I hadn't come home, that I had deserted them?

In God's name, what had happened to me?

I felt like a fly wrapped up in the invisible web of some unseen spider—the accident with its shocking revelation, the in-
cident on the porch, the abrupt shift to the cell. . . .

Meaningless. It was like one of Kit's games with Silky, the
yellow-and-black striped tiger, Pinky, the dog whose fur was
now more gray than pink, Pandy. . . . "Now we're on a
train," he'd say. "We're going to Grammy's, and I'm the engineer. . . . We're there. You're a tiger, Silky, and you're in
the jungle, and I'm going to kill you. . . . Mommy, I want a
drink. . . ."

And there they would sit, lifeless where he had left them,
the reproved and the punished, the hunted, the companions,
and the finally cuddled, until he returned to take up the game
again as if nothing had happened. Did they wonder, these
tormented toys, at the sudden changes, the inexplicable
shifts, the childish moods that switched with the wind?

Did they wonder where Kit had gone? No. For them nothing happened except when Kit was there. Time was only
when Kit willed there to be time; the game didn't start until
he said, "Begin!"

He would be missing Brownie.

When would I see Kit again?

A wave of grief swept through me, and I covered my face
with my hand. My thought at the accident came back: *Somebody slipped.* Why had the cop echoed it: *Somebody sure
slipped on this one?*

Crazy, crazy.

I was the unwitting, central figure in some vast, in-
comprehensible plot. Behind it was someone who knew why
the woman hit by the truck had been stuffed with sawdust
and excelsior.

I wouldn't give up, I thought. I'd fight Them.

I started going through my clothes. I found my pocket
knife in my right-hand pants' pocket. That was the only thing
they had left me. It was odd they hadn't taken it away.

Maybe they had missed it. Or maybe it was one of those
things that show up in spite of searches. Prisoners are always

coming up with unexpected things: knives, poison, saws, guns. . . .

I started honing the blade methodically on the sole of my shoe, staring down
(   )
at the lean jailor. Sawdust and excelsior were spilling through a hole in his chest.

I felt as though
(   )
the courtroom was crowded even before I turned to look behind. I was sitting at a dark, highly polished table. In front of me was a judge behind his high desk. A witness was in the chair to his left. He was a middle-aged man I'd never seen before.

Against the wall to my right was the jury, twelve sober men and women met to decide whether someone was guilty or innocent, listening intently to the testimony. . . .

I shook my head in bewilderment. It had happened again, twice. What had made the hole in the jailor's chest? The knife I had been sharpening? What had happened after I stood over his body, shocked, immobile, watching the stuffing mound up on the floor?

The man beside me was Orin Porter, the lawyer I would have if I ever needed a lawyer. "What's happening?" I said. "Get me out of here!"

"Shhhh!" he cautioned, a finger to his lips. He nodded toward the witness box and the jury.

". . . and I saw this man push the woman in front of the truck," the witness was saying earnestly.

Standing near him was a dapper little man in a gray pin-stripe suit. Lawyer? Prosecutor? "Did you ever see the man before?"

"No, sir."

"Have you seen him since?"

"Yes, sir."

"Where?"

"Here—in this courtroom."

"Can you point him out?"

"Yes, sir. That's him. That's the man." The finger of the

witness pointed straight at me.

It lifted me out of my chair, protesting. "I didn't push anybody," I shouted. "I don't know what you're talking—"

Porter yanked me down hard. "Shut up!" he said. "You'll prejudice the judge—"

"The defendant will control himself or the court will be forced to do it for him," the judge said coldly. He was a narrow-faced, intolerant man. His eyes were too close together, and he was determined that I should hang.

Only they didn't hang people any more. Not in this state.

I hated him, knowing that it was ridiculous. "But I didn't push anybody," I whispered to Porter. "If they're talking about that accident, I was just a witness—"

"You've been positively identified six times," Porter said softly, frowning. "Five of the witnesses saw you push the girl."

"But I didn't even know her. I had no reason—"

"It's been established that you've visited the girl's apartment several times when you were supposed to be working." A flicker of distaste broke through Porter's professional neutrality. "Jane's broken up about it."

"Mad, mad," I whispered, staring blankly into the distance. "Have they brought out the part about the sawdust?"

"Sawdust?"

"The sawdust and excelsior that came out of the woman, the stuffing—"

Porter studied me for a moment before he said, "Maybe you're right. An insanity plea is your only hope."

"What about the jailor?" I pleaded. "Did he die? Are they going to do anything about him?"

"What jailor?" Porter asked, his eyebrows compressed. "Are you holding something back?"

I shook my head and sank back in my chair. Life had suddenly become a twisted thing that could never be straightened out again into sanity. I was on trial for pushing into the path of a truck a woman I had never seen. And the jailor was forgotten.

I needed some kind of explanation, but the only possible explanation was too terrible to entertain. If I wasn't mad, then someone was framing me with incredible efficiency for a crime I didn't commit.

Why? There could only be one reason: I had seen the accident and recognized the truth about the woman who was killed. I knew she wasn't human.

Who was framing me was the unanswerable part. Because anyone who could frame me like this, who could convince a dozen witnesses that they had seen something they couldn't have seen, who could identify me when no one knew my name, who could shift me through space and time—why, He was beyond identification and His reasons were beyond understanding.

Call it the supernatural and let it go. Terror lurked behind it. But it explained everything so well: I had stumbled on a secret that no one was supposed to know, the secret that some of us aren't human, aren't real, that some of us—the girl, the jailor—are stuffed with sawdust and excelsior like teddy bears, that even the real ones are moved about by godlike beings for reasons we could never understand.

And, having stumbled on this basic truth, I had to die or be so discredited that my revelations would be discounted as madness or a self-serving simulation of it.

I looked around the courtroom. Anyone might be a puppet, a teddy bear, the witnesses who came to the chair and lied, the jury
                    (   )
will consider its verdict," the judge said grimly.

I hardly noticed the shifts any more. My fantastic speculations went on uninterrupted.

Fantastic, but not so hard to believe. The theory explained the observable facts of existence as well as our naive realism. What do we know, really? Only what we are told. And what we are told has no inevitable correlation with reality.

Why couldn't people be stuffed? I'd never seen an operation or an autopsy. All I knew about the interior of the human body was hearsay and the vague consciousness of my own inner workings.

Was it incredible that there should be teddy bears among us, moved willy-nilly at the whim of supernatural beings? Was it fantastic that the whole world should be the stage for extra-dimensional puppeteers? Yes, yes it was. But no more incredible, no more fantastic than what had happened to me.

A workable hypothesis has to account for every fact, and only mine accounted for these shattering experiences.

"All the world's a stage," said Shakespeare, but it needn't be so vast an enterprise. What did I know of other cities, foreign lands? I had visited some of them, sure—or, at least, I had the memory, which isn't necessarily the same thing—but how little of it I had sensed myself. It was only an infinitesimal part of what I was asked to believe.

I accepted China on faith and India and all the vast teeming East. Perhaps Africa was only fiction and the menace of Iron-Curtained Russia. There was no trustworthy proof that Australia really existed or Europe or even England. . . .

The testimony of maps was the chief evidence for the reality of much of the United States, and only history books propagated the illusion that the world had existed before my consciousness. . . .

And what of memory, a poor, fallible thing as we all knew? Surely, it was obvious, now, that memories can be planted in people's minds like tulip bulbs in flower beds. Let those who think they have special knowledge of this fact or that, of the nature of the world or the workings of the human body, which will shatter my feeble cosmogony—let them reflect on the elusive origins of memory and the success of even we inept mortals in hypnosis and psychiatry and brain-washings. . . .

And I must be immune from this tyranny of memory because I am real, I thought. *I am human, and that is why my knowledge is dangerous.*

And the thoughts proved my reality, my humanity, because surely a teddy bear can think only those thoughts that are thought for him.

Teddy bear. I looked in the chair beside me, and there was Brownie, still wearing the handkerchief around his middle. I picked him up; my probing finger found the gash.

That hadn't changed. Well, why should it? Which would have been proof of my suspicions: Brownie slashed or Brownie whole?

I shook my head angrily. There was no way of proving anything. I was trapped, hopelessly; I might as well surrender to whatever fate was planned. A man can't fight the gods.

I stuck my hands deep in my pockets and touched the knife. I pulled it out and snapped open the blade. It was sharp, honed, much sharper than I'd ever kept it. A few bits of sawdust clung to the blade.

Proof! Maybe not to anybody else, but to me. They couldn't think of everything. They made mistakes. And it was the little inconsistencies of life we dismiss so casually that were the ultimate and unshakable proof that we are not the masters of our world or of our fates.

Our hypothesis about existence was really a shaky structure, shot full of holes, tottering on a patchwork foundation of faith. Take the inexplicable. Its existence is proof that the world is not a world of order, that nature is not understandable and subject to law.

In such a world of order and law, nothing should be inexplicable. There should be no such mysterious disappearances as those of Ambrose Bierce and Judge Crater. (Had they learned too much?) There should be no mysterious appearances of men who are dead or long lost, who should be gone forever. But Enoch Arden returns—so often that we need an Enoch Arden law to protect the "widow."

The small things—that is where the game is exposed if we would only notice. Things are not where they should be, or they are found where they should not be. We forget how often it happens because the things are little: clothing, toys, supplies, implements. . . . Knives disappear, and needles, spools, and spatulas; socks vanish, and buttons, cuff links, and belts; marbles are gone, and jacks, tops, and checkers; staples never diminish gradually—suddenly the cupboard is bare.

Poor Mother Hubbard. Pitiful dog.

Other things: paper clips, clothes hangers, rubber bands, string, pencils, wrapping paper, glue, nails, screws. . . . One person may find them always at hand although he never buys any of them. Another may buy these things constantly and never find any when he wants them.

Explain it! Shrug? Indict human memory? Exalt the supremacy of *things?* There's a better explanation: carelessness.

Not *our* carelessness. *Theirs.*

All the world's a stage,
And all the men and women merely players . . .

and the play is too vast and obscure for us ever to understand. It isn't surprising that the minor props go astray. The Director may not be a Belasco. The Property Manager can distribute too many paper clips here, too many pencils there, with a fine contempt for the ability of the actors to trust their own senses and memories over the pseudo-solidity of "reality."

Why has no science of psychology ever been developed? Why does a workable science of sociology seem impossible? Because of the teddy bears. The logic of their actions is never a human logic but an extra-human whimsy. The picture is blurred.

Let some thinker devise a great, logical system which will encompass the whole of human behavior, which will predict behavior and explain the past—and the exceptions will come bobbing up to laugh the theory into oblivion.

Why do so many people refuse to be swayed by logic? Why do so many misguided idiots cling stubbornly to their false values, call their demagogues saviors, start fights and riots and mob violence and wars?

Teddy bears. Puppets manipulated by the invisible puppeteers. Judas goats leading the sheep into the slaughterhouse. The mob pressing humanity behind, forcing us forward into darkness and pain and distrust.

I slid the knife along my arm and watched the thin, red line follow behind it, broadening as the blood welled. I sighed. At least I wasn't one of the teddy bears.

Porter was staring down at my arm and the knife in my hand. "For God's sake, man," he whispered fiercely, "put that thing away!"

But the foreman of the jury was speaking. "Guilty," he said, and the judge
(   )
felt limp and lifeless under my left hand, clutching his shoulder. I was standing behind him, my right hand over the judge's shoulder, pressed to his robe, and I was looking out over the court and all the white, horrified faces.

One of them I knew. It was paler than all the rest, and the anguish in it was like a knife blade inside me. I stepped back.

The knife in my right hand came away. The judge, released, toppled slowly, turning a little in his chair. His thin, vindictive face was relaxed; his close-set eyes unseeing.

Sawdust streamed out of the slit beneath his vest.

I started forward blindly toward Jane, in spite of the uniforms that rose in front of me, and the hands that clutched at me to hold me back, and I

(   )

was lying flat on the ground. It was night, and I was cold. The earth was cold under me, cold against my shirt, against my thin trousers, and I wondered where I was.

Bushes were in front of me, branching darkly against the night. As I reached out to part them, I realized that the knife was still in my hand. I closed it and put it away.

Something furry was beside me. Brownie. I smiled grimly. I could lose everything else, innocence, responsibility, love, life . . . but I couldn't lose Brownie. It was comforting to have him there.

I understood now why Kit couldn't go to sleep without his friend. Whatever terrifying shapes and places contorted the protean night, Brownie was the familiar, unchanging earth to which a frightened child could cling.

Kit and I, frightened children both.

Dimly, from a corner, beamed a street light, and I recognized the winding street now. Porter's house was the nearest one, there with the light in the living room behind the picture window. That man in the chair, reading, that must be Orin.

Whatever the risk, I realized that I had to see him. I had to know what had happened.

I crept between the bushes, and their bristles and brambles shredded my flimsy illusion of nightmare with their rough reality. I crept forward, keeping in the shadows, watchful for movements or darkened cars, edging toward the two-foot square slab of concrete that served the ranch-style house as porch.

I punched the bell and turned my back to the screen so that I could watch the dark street, feeling like a character in a B-grade gangster movie.

The door opened. I turned. It was Orin, the light haloing

his head. He blinked into the darkness. "Who is it?" he
asked, and flipped on the little porch light. "Jimmie!" he
gasped. Hastily he pushed open the screen. "Get in here!"
I sank wearily into a chair in the living room. Orin pulled
the draw drapes across the picture window and turned to me
impatiently. I sat heavily, hugging Brownie to me, feeling a
little foolish. "What's happened?" I asked.

"Judge Marsh died twenty minutes ago. The police are
turning the city upside down. They have orders to shoot if
there's a chance you might escape—"

"How did I escape from the courtroom?"

"Don't you remember?" Porter exclaimed.

"The last I remember a dozen men were reaching for me."

Porter shook his head in disbelief. "I can't understand how
you got this far out. Your picture is all over town—a taxi
wouldn't carry you or a bus—and it's almost ten miles. You
didn't walk, did you?"

"I don't know," I said wearily. "They've shifted me around
too much. You saw the judge, I guess. You saw the sawdust
spilling out of him?"

Porter stared at me with eyes that were suddenly wise.
"You are crazy, aren't you?" he whispered.

"No," I said quickly. "It's not me. It's"—words weren't
equal to the task of explaining what had happened, of con-
vincing Porter—"you wouldn't believe me."

"I'll fix you a drink," he said quickly, heading for the kitch-
en. "Come on. It'll do you good. Then you're going to give
yourself up. Don't worry—we'll get you off—"

"No! That's what they want."

"Come on. We'll talk about it."

He made the drink strong and tall and cool and left me
with it. I sipped it numbly, trying to make sense out of insanity.

Maybe it's like Miguel de Unamuno speculated, I thought.
What was his remarkable question: Is the whole world—and
we with it—only a dream of God? Are prayer and ritual nothing but attempts to make Him more drowsy so that He
doesn't wake up and stop our dreaming?

But if this is all our existence, to call it a dream can't diminish its importance. Dreams can bleed. I proved that.

I looked at my arm. A thin, white scar crossed it. That was quick healing. Another slip?

I took out the knife again and opened the blade and tapped the handle against my palm. Sawdust. The blade itself was untarnished, unstained. Surely, if the judge and the jailor had been real, their blood would have rusted the blade.

Only how could I convince anyone else? They would see Brownie, and their cynical wisdom would know where the sawdust came from.

Porter had been gone a long time. I got up, the knife forgotten in my hand, and pushed through the door and surprised him. He had the telephone to his ear, and his eyes were frightened before he veiled them. He said, "Well, that's all right, then. Thanks for calling."

He was lying. The phone hadn't rung.

I moved toward him, hurt, aching. "I didn't think you'd turn me in," I said distantly.

"I didn't," he said weakly. "I swear I didn't, Jimmie. I wouldn't do anything—"

"You shouldn't have done that, Orin. If you only knew what I've gone through—"

"Put the knife away," he said, his voice strained and off-key. "You don't need the knife. You'll hurt—"

I looked down at the knife in my hand, and he sprang at me. The movement startled me. Instinctively, I moved aside. He plunged onto the knife.

His face worked for a moment close to mine, trying to get out words through a strangled throat, and a spasm of pain crossed his face, and he collapsed sideways, pulling free of the knife.

How easily they die, I thought dully. *You wouldn't think a teddy bear would die so easily.*

From the slash across his belly came a thin sifting of yellow saw

( )

dust rose from my running feet. I could feel it deep in my lungs, and it sifted through the air, diffusing the radiance of the street light ahead. I was fleeing through an alley, unpaved and rough under my feet.

"Stop!" bellowed a voice behind me. "Stop, you!"

I didn't stop. A moment later, almost simultaneously, a gun barked and a bullet whined past my head. I dodged, panting, into a dark yard, ducking clothes lines and avoiding the dark traps of bushes with an odd prescience until I reached the narrow walk between houses and raced through it.

"Stop!" the voice yelled again.

But I had lost him. I eased, lungs burning, into a trot and went down a driveway onto a sidewalk. The neighborhood was anonymous in the night. It could have been any older collection of five-room bungalows and thirty-foot frontages. When I reached the corner I would find out.

If I wasn't crazy, that is. I thought maybe I was crazy, after all. We've all had the thought that we were all alone against a hostile world, that we were the only real person in a make-believe world, that unseen, malicious forces are combined against us. . . . That's the common delusion of adolescence, and it fades.

But when the delusion becomes systematized, and the senses begin to support it with false messages. . . . Oh, my case was a classic description of paranoia: exaggerated suspicion leading to a lasting, immovable, delusional system of persecution and grandeur. . . .

Also, homicidal.

The only trouble with the theory was that I wanted too much to believe it. I would rather be insane than have my speculations true. It had to be one or the other, and I would rather believe that I was crazy than that everybody but me was a *thing* stuffed with sawdust and maneuvered by some supernatural or extra-dimensional intelligence to trap me into something monstrous and unthinkable. . . .

But why? Only I couldn't ever expect to know. The motives of the supernatural must be inexplicable, or it would be natural.

So it was either one or the other, and I thought: *Let me be mad!*

But the thought was too sane.

I hesitated at the corner, under the street light, and I looked up at the sign. Before I could read it, a beam of light blazed into my eyes.

I clenched them tight and hid behind my arm, realizing

only then that Brownie was dangling by one leg from my hand. I spun away.

"Stop!" said an amplified voice. "Don't move. This is the police."

I ran, dodging quickly up a flight of steps, across a lawn, and up on a porch while the spotlight tried vainly to find me and the loudspeaker roared.

Where are the people who live inside, I thought wildly, *or is it only a false front like a movie set, and there's nobody behind it? All false fronts?* . . .

And I hammered on the strange front
(   )
door, only it wasn't strange after all. It was my own front door, and the street behind me was quiet, dark, and deserted.

The living room light came on, and through the fog of curtain behind the pane of the front door I saw Jane coming toward me, pulling a robe around her. She opened the front door until it was stopped by the night chain. "Who is it?" she asked, and then, "It's you!"

I pulled open the screen and pushed my way into the house. It was good to be home, even as a fugitive. I wasn't going to run any more. Let them come and get me here. I was through with the long torment of fighting Them.

I dropped into my own deep chair and sighed and lowered my face into my hands. *Let it be a dream!* I prayed.

After a moment I took my hands away and looked at Jane. Her face told me the truth.

"So it really happened," I said.

"Yes. You're crazy, aren't you?"

"I suppose so," I agreed wearily. "That's the best explanation, isn't it?"

She nodded and turned her face away. The light from the red lamp glittered on the unspilled teardrops in her eyes. She wiped them away. "I can't understand," she said. "I've tried but I can't—that woman, then the judge, then your best friend—"

"Stuffed," I mused. "All stuffed. The jailor, too. Teddy bears." I looked down at Brownie. He had come with me through everything. I pulled the handkerchief free and held him out to Jane. "Sew him up," I said. "I don't want Kit to see him like that."

She took the teddy bear and looked at the slit across his abdomen. "No," she said softly, "that would be the worst."
She thought I'd done it. A denial rose to my lips, but I
forced it back. What difference did it make? "Where is Kit?"
"I sent him over to your mother's. I didn't think it would
be good for him here."

Or safe, I thought. "But you stayed."

"I thought you'd come home if you could."

"Yes." I watched her sew up the slit neatly with brown
thread. Soon it would be done. I wished all things could be
mended as easily. I wished I could tell her what had happened to me. No use. "You won't turn me in, will you?"

"No. It won't be necessary. They've been watching the
house. Before they come, will you tell me why?"

"No. If you're one of the teddy bears, it doesn't matter. If
you're one of the humans, it might condemn you to what I've
gone through."

"You're talking nonsense," she said, biting off the thread.

I sighed. "All right. Some people are real—some are only
stuffed like Brownie, there. Filled with sawdust and excelsior,
shoved around in some great, extra-dimensional game by
things moving behind the scenes who are masters of time and
space. Crazy, isn't it? But that's the way things are."

She smiled contemptuously. "It's easy enough to prove I'm
real. Give me your knife."

I opened it for her and handed it to her. I waited for
her to cut her arm as I did. But, with a superior smile,
she plunged the knife into her abdomen.

My hand went viciously over my eyes, clawing at my face
to shut out the sight. But the image was imprinted indelibly
on my retina: the look of surprise on her face and the sawdust
that flew dustily where the knife had entered.

And I knew, finally, what the truth was.

It was the first really crazy thing that anyone else had done.
It was senseless by any standards. Jane hadn't known she was
a teddy bear. Someone had pulled her string. And there was
no possible reason for it.

There was, when I thought back, no satisfactory reason for

anything They had done. They didn't need to do all this to silence me. That was an easy thing for masters of time and space, unworthy of all the troubles to set up this scene and all the others.

I knew the reason now, and it was more horrible than anything I had thought of before: Amusement.

It had been a game, a grisly sort of game of blind man's buff with a knife in my hand and my eyes opened too wide. . . .

It was the sort of game a child would play with his stuffed animals. We were the nursery toys for an extra-dimensional child. We were his teddy bears, performing for his amusement. Maybe he learned something from us.

Maybe we weren't that important.

Possibly there came times in the game when the extra-dimensional adults stepped in, when the child grew too abandoned, when the teddy bears were in danger of complete destruction. Maybe they fixed everything up again, just as Jane had mended Brownie. . . .

The light burned against the front door, and the voice boomed from the loudspeaker in the street: "Come out, Gunn! We know you're in there!"

"All right," I muttered. "I'm coming. I'm coming."

The question was: Could a man rebel?

I found the gun in Kit's toy chest and stepped to the front door and opened it, squinting my eyes against the glare. With a quick flip of my wrist, I raised the revolver into view. The chatter of the machine gun was violence in the street.

The slugs stitched their way across my side. I felt them battering as I toppled slowly, my hand cupped to the pain. It caught the sawdust as it trickled onto

(   )

the porch, and I stopped, my hand pressed to the stitch in my side. I took a deep breath and thought ruefully that I wasn't as young as I used to be. I was going to have to start taking those steps a little slower.

My foot sank into something soft. I pulled back and felt foolish. I knew what it was.

Lying on the cement of the porch, his sliding black pupils intent in their plastic corneas as he tried to understand the stars, was Brownie—Kit's teddy bear.

I picked him up. Jane had done a good job on the slit in his abdomen where Kit had played doctor the other day. He wouldn't do that again. He understood now that toys were to play with, not to destroy, and that someday he might do something we couldn't fix.

I wished for a moment that I was a child again and could have all my tattered illusions made whole as easily.

But I shrugged and opened the door and said, "Jane, Kit, I'm home," like it didn't happen every evening.

5. *The Man Who Owned Tomorrow*

HE WAS the saddest man I ever saw.

I was young then, just starting practice as a psychologist, and I often played a game with myself, trying to guess the profession of my patients before they spoke. *A professor,* I thought, *in some quiet, ivy-covered college. Or a businessman, most at home in a dark-paneled conference room. Or a doctor, not a general practicioner but a specialist—a surgeon, perhaps.*

From his physical appearance, I judged him to be about fifty. He was tall, slim, and excellently dressed in a conservative business suit, a white shirt, a dark four-in-hand. His hair was white at the temples, though a darker gray above; his face was firm, lightly tanned, and lined as if with pain. But his eyes were incredibly old.

Everything else was a mask through which his eyes looked out upon the world. And the world looked at his eyes and could not look away, because they held the world's misery and a sorrow for it beyond imagining.

His eyes were dark and depthless. I stared into them for a long time, longer than was polite, longer than was wise.

"Yes," he said, as if confirming a previous impression. "Yes," he said again, but more softly this time, with pity in it.

He sank down in a chair opposite my desk and closed his eyes. I looked away. When I looked back at him I had myself under control.

"I am going to tell you something I have never told anyone before," he said wearily. "I can read the future."

I nodded tactfully. "I shall respect your confidence. Can you do this any time you wish or is it dependent upon conditions?"

"Any time," he said. "Or, rather, always."

"What is the difference?"

"It is independent of my desires," he said wistfully. "It is like seeing when you open your eyes."

"Were you born with this ability," I asked, "or did it develop?"

He hesitated for only a moment. "I suppose you would call it a gift."

"It must be a very convenient ability to have," I commented drily.

"One would think so." He smiled ruefully. "However, I do not speak of the general future but of the individual futures of everyone I meet."

I settled back in my chair. "You can read my future then?"

"Oh, yes," he said.

I leaned forward. "Tell me."

"That," he said, "is what I came here to do."

This is what he told me:

My story begins, I suppose, with a man dying in a gypsy tent near a small Magyar village. He died with a knife in his back, writhing in agony, but in his eyes was a look of peace I never hope to see again.

For I saw him die. I was twenty-two. I had just graduated from college, and my uncle, who was my guardian, had given me an extended tour of Europe as a graduation present. I cut short my trip and returned home. Most of the trip I spent alone, locked in a compartment, a suite, a stateroom.

At first I was frequently nauseated. From everyone I looked at streamed a succession of figures and scenes only slightly less real than the person himself, fading as they receded, with here and there a scene which was firm and definite. The future is not fixed. Everyone has an infinite number of choices, but they vary in probability. The less probable paths are vague and indistinct. But the future is strongly governed by causality, the strongest factor of which is the nature of the person himself. Some future events are almost unchangeable. Paths lead there from all points of departure.

But, as I was saying, I had difficulty in distinguishing between the reality of the present moment and the probabilties of the future. Often I was forced to lie down in my room. But after several months my senses and my mind adjusted themselves to their new existence.

I became fascinated by my new ability. I mingled with comparatively wealthy people who were less liable to temptation, serious illness, violence, or tragedy. The majority of the secrets I learned were only pleasantly titillating. I felt quite godlike in my knowledge, and I enjoyed a considerable vogue as a fortune-teller at parties.

At one evening gathering, a beautiful young girl approached the table where I was being all-wise. Gaily she sat down to have her fortune told, but I gasped and ran from the room. I forced myself to return later and make my excuses. I could not, of course, tell her the true reason. Every choice in her future led to death within a year by a malignant growth already at work within her. I have never told another fortune.

I returned to college and enrolled in medical school. I never went home again. Old friends had begun to be uneasy around me. And I could not be natural toward them. I knew too much about them; my fortune-telling had been too accurate. More important, I had already entered another world. On the streets I would pass strangers in all walks of life who would impress their fates on my consciousness: Here a man destined for maiming by the machine he tended, there a man who was going to murder his wife. Fraud, theft, embezzlement; seduction, adultery, incest, rape; violence, disease, death. . . .

There was nothing I could do. I avoided the streets; I lived alone. I had begun to realize the terrible price of my foreknowledge.

After receiving my degree, I set up practice in this city. I specialized in diagnostics. It was a natural choice; no other doctor could compare with me. A fraction of my time I devoted to a wealthy clientele. From them I made enough to spend the remainder with free clinic patients. Whenever a course of treatment would be successful, I knew it. If the patient was incurable, I could help him to the choice which would best prepare him and his family for it.

It was not always so clear-cut. There were times when recovery by a patient would lead only to tragedy for himself or others. A child, if it lived, was doomed to imbecility. A man would later die a lingering death of multiple sclerosis. A woman would kill her child and then herself. A man would assassinate a public figure. What should I do?

I refused to be God. All such cases I turned over to other doctors without comment, to live or die as someone or something else should decide. Perhaps I was wrong.

I have resisted the impulse to interfere in public events. By a suggestion here, an action there, I could have changed the course of history. But I could never see far enough. I could never see the future whole. The world I shaped might know a little joy and an overpowering weight of tragedy, or a brief moment of peace and infinity of grief. I was not wise enough. Perhaps I was wrong here, too.

Often my life has been unbearable; always it has been miserable. My life, I say—and yet I have had no life. My only personal function has been to keep alive and in circumstances necessary for what I had to do. I had no friends, no wife, no children. I was too different, too strange. And I could love no one. I knew too much. If I were too close I would try to move them out of the way of unhappiness and disaster. Soon or late, that becomes impossible, and attempting it would keep me so busy that I would have time for nothing else. Soon they would have no lives of their own; they would be automatons, moving at my whim. They would sense it. Before long they would hate me. Eventually they would try to kill me. Impersonal grief is bad enough; personal tragedy cannot be endured for long.

I learned my lesson early. The girl doomed with cancer was my fiancée.

Many times I thought of suicide. But I could see that it was not in my future. I have gone so far as to raise a gun to my head in defiance, but I could never pull the trigger. Even in this small way I could not participate in life. My role was inescapable; I was a spectator at life.

Spectator at misery. In every life, no matter how placid,

how uneventful, how sheltered, misery lies in wait. And with it agony, despair, and death. Everywhere and forever. I have seen it all. Happiness is fleeting. Sorrow is eternal.

Why could I not kill myself? Perhaps because in my pain I relieved the world's pain a little. I helped my patients and I helped humanity in general. I have seen many diseases; I have seen their underlying causes; I have seen the treatment to which the patient will best respond. Reluctant to call attention to myself, I have guided other men to important discoveries—with articles, speeches, lectures, suggestions—always so subtly that they could not be traced to me. It is not wise to appear too knowing; strangely enough, this gift is envied.

And yet I have not been able to do as much as I once thought possible. In many cases a cure was not indicated; all the patient's lines led to death. For these, the world was not ready to supply a cure; the man was not yet born who would discover the drug or the treatment; the technical level of civilization was too low to manufacture the necessities or support the process. So it is with cancer and others.

I am convinced that no disease is and always will be fatal, even senility. I have seen the life span lengthened considerably during my time; even more will be done during yours.

The old gypsy fortune-teller who passed on to me this ability was more courageous than I; he had sought to change the course of Europe. Whether he did well or ill I do not know. In the end he died beneath a paid assassin's knife.

I have often wondered what would have happened to me if I had not entered his tent. But experience has taught me that I could not have avoided my fate. He knew he was about to die.

Two weeks ago a man came to my office for diagnosis. He posed as a businessman, but I saw that he was actually the leader of a criminal organization grown rich and powerful through evasion of the Volstead Act. He was suffering from an obscure but painful and ultimately fatal disease, which does not yet even have a name. I could have cured him, but the price was misery, agony, and death for many others. I told him I could not help. He is a vicious, violent man; he will be executed six months from now for murder.

Immediately afterward, my own choices narrowed down to only a few. All of them led here.

"And that is why," he said, "I have come to you."

"That is very interesting," I said, "but I thought you were going to tell me my future."

"That is your future," he said. "Look!"

He stared at me. His eyes were large and deep black and bottomless. My office faded away. I seemed to be diving deep into twin pools of darkness, down, down, down. . . .

"Look," said someone far away.

"No," I tried to shout. "No!" But I could not speak. I tried to close my eyes. They would not shut. I could not move. I felt nothing.

I looked. My head seemed to swell outward to encompass the whole room. And then it shrank back to its normal size, and I was in my body again, and it was under my control. All except my eyes. They saw too much.

The room was full of people, crowding in upon me, everywhere, smothering. I could not breathe. All of the people were me. I screamed.

"Look!" he said again.

I looked. He was not one man but several. Images radiated out from him in all directions, like bicycle spokes. Only one of the lines had any duration. I followed it. Fighting, against my will, I watched him walk out of my office, through the waiting room, and down the hall. I saw him enter the elevator and descend to the street level, go through the front door, cross the street.

A long black car, parked down the street, pulled away from the curb. A white hand emerged from the car window, holding something dark and shiny. The car came abreast. The dark, shiny object jerked twice. Smoke spurted. He staggered and slowly crumpled to the sidewalk. The car jumped forward and disappeared in a blue swirl of exhaust. . . .

I closed my eyes.

"Now," he said gently, "it is yours."

I opened my eyes for a moment and then shut them tightly. I felt nauseated. "I don't want it," I said faintly.

"No one does," he said. "But it is a gift that cannot be refused. Always there is one who must have it."

"Why?"

"I do not know, but the paths are clear. When the paths come to a halt for one of us, they center first on someone else. When you have lived with it as long as I have, you will know that some things cannot be evaded."

"There must be a reason," I said. I spoke from a world of darkness. I would not open my eyes. "It must have started somewhere."

"The origins are lost," he said. "It has been a long, long time. The gypsy did not know. But there are legends. Wise men, ahead of their time, who were feared, hated, betrayed. There is the story of the Wandering Jew. There was a man named Jesus. He is said to have done many strange things. He cured the incurable. He could foretell the future."

"But why?" I said between clenched teeth. "Why?"

"I have wondered, too. Is it planned by some other intelligence, which lays down the paths we see? Or was it an accidental discovery? Did some ancient seeker into the unknown blunder into it and find himself trapped? It will give you an interesting distraction from other thoughts. I tend, myself, toward a plan. We have great capacity for doing good. It is as great as our capacity for suffering."

"The scapegoat!" I groaned.

"Perhaps. It is an eternal human necessity. Lay the tribe's sins upon the god and stone him to death. But on the other hand, we may be a different type of goat—the Judas goat that leads the sheep into the slaughterhouse. Only it doesn't have to be the slaughterhouse. We can lead the way toward a better world and a better race. I think, on the whole, that we have. Perhaps we are the one consciously directive force in the world, saving civilization from dropping back into primeval savagery. Perhaps we are the world's conscience."

"You forced this on me. Can it be given to anyone?" I asked him.

"I do not know. I have never tried. Nowhere, except in your case, was it in a person's possible future. And I have never had the callousness or temerity to experiment. But if you are considering giving it to others in order to have companionship, remember this: They will hate you, just as you hate me. For me, it does not matter. But you must live, and you will be able to foresee the inevitable result. And to know the consequences of evil is fatal to the act."

"I don't believe you," I said savagely. "It is all a trick. Hypnotism. Illusion."

He was silent.

"Get out," I said. I lowered my head to the desk. I heard him get up.

"I am going," he said. "You see, we cannot be friends, even though we bear the same gift—or curse. I think, on the whole, I have been too timid. The world is in need of guidance. Learn as much as you can. Grow wise. Use your power well. And God help you."

I heard him leave. One door opened and closed. And another. After a pause, I heard the elevator door open and slide shut again. Then silence.

I got up, my eyes still closed. I walked to the window and pressed my forehead to it and opened my eyes. Looking outside, it was not so bad. There were no radiating shapes out there, and five floors below, the street was almost deserted.

He came out the door and walked across the street steadily, not looking up.

A long black car, parked down the street, pulled away from the curb. A white hand emerged from the car window, holding something dark and shiny. The car came abreast. The dark, shiny object jerked twice. Smoke spurted. He staggered and slowly crumpled to the sidewalk. The car jumped forward and disappeared in a blue swirl of exhaust. . . .

I went back to my desk with my eyes closed and sat down and lowered my head to rest it against my folded arms. I heard the door open.

"Doctor," my receptionist said, "is there something wrong? Are you ill?"

I raised my head and opened my eyes. Her figure swayed dizzily in front of me.

"Yes," I said, gritting my teeth. "I feel a little ill. I will see no one else today. I think I will not see anyone else for some time. Will you take care of it?"

"Yes, Doctor," she said. She came closer. "Is there anything I can do?"

I tried to focus my eyes. I saw her a little more clearly,
young, light-haired, very beautiful. And one path led toward
a church. It was a strong path, but as I watched, it began to
fade.

"No," I said. "Nothing. I am going to close the office. You
will have no difficulty in finding another job, I know, but I
will give you two months' wages in lieu of notice."

"But—" she began, startled and close to tears.

"Please go now," I said.

The path I was watching disappeared.

That was twenty-five years ago.

"And that is why," I said, "I have come to you."

You are thinking, I know, that I am the saddest man you
ever saw.

6. *Green Thumb*

JOHNNY SUNDANCE *was seven parts Cherokee Indian and one part tramp printer. He was born in 1972 at the Chilocco Indian School, Oklahoma, where his father taught mathematics.*

Johnny's father was all Cherokee, with a Cherokee's fierce pride and a Cherokee's stoicism. When he discovered what his child was, he poured his frustrated ambition and his knowledge into Johnny as his ancestors had once poured powder into a trade musket.

Johnny learned to read when he was three. When he was five he was reading all the books in his father's library, and his father started him on algebra.

His parents died in the last of the great airplane crashes, before automatic avoidance mechanisms became compulsory. They had a reservation on an earlier plane, but their helicab had been trapped in a Los Angeles traffic jam.

Johnny was six years old.

The government put him into a primary grade pool in a modern school at the Haskell Indian Institute. He graduated to the fourth grade at seven, began his scientific education at eight, and advanced at his own best speed until he graduated from high school at eleven, from college at fourteen, got his Ph.D. at sixteen, and passed his boards the same year.

He was a specialist. Those qualified to judge his work considered him the most brilliant quantum physicist in the country.

He won his first contest at nine with an original paper on atomic models. In the years following he published five books on particle physics and innumerable articles in scholarly journals.

He liked poetry, beer, and mountain climbing.
Just after his nineteenth birthday, he disappeared.

The type bars slamming viciously through the ribbon and paper against the hard rubber platen made the old-fashioned typewriter jump on the cluttered solid walnut desk. Gideon McKenzie glared at the paper as his stubby fingers jabbed at the keys. Occasionally a distant clink of metal against metal made him twitch, miss a key, and swear.

"The principle of specialization became inextricably embedded in the social matrix during the late 1960's," he wrote.

"It was based on a recognition of the green thumb phenomenon: everyone has a talent which needs only the proper environment of social approval, favorable circumstances, and frequent, much admired successes to develop genius out of what may be only superior original capacity. It was at once the salvation and the curse of Twentieth Century civilization.

"The arguments for it went like this: you can't have a complex civilization without specialists; knowledge has become too extensive for any one man to encompass it all. It's as much as he can do to master one small aspect of a subject. When there was much to learn, a spade was sufficient, but now that all the ground has been turned over, a man must dig deep to find virgin soil. He needs a sharpshooter.

"What has been called a revolution is actually the maturation of tendencies evident in the early years of the Electronic Age, and this is a lot of over-ripe manure!"

Gideon jerked the paper out of the typewriter, crumpling it in his hand, and glowered at the machine as if it were to blame. A McKenzie glare was a terrifying thing, but a glower was enough to freeze even a typewriter's bearings.

Gideon was a lumpy man. He looked like he had been molded in a bass fiddle case and then a clumsy child had stuck on fat blobs for legs and arms. But his face was his own creation. Once it had been fat and jolly, but it had been carved by indignation and mottled by choler. The nose was a piece of red-veined putty; his eyebrows were dark bushes under which his pale blue eyes lurked in wait for the unwary bungler. His hair was thick, black, and unkempt, like a nest he had slept in.

The typewriter waited, unmoved, amid the precarious stacks of dusty books and tattered manuscripts on the desk. Gideon rolled another sheet of paper into the machine and began to pound the keys again. When he finished, he drew the sheet carefully out of the typewriter, and leaning back in the wooden desk chair read it with an expression of Machiavellian delight.

Dear Barney:
I have written many potboilers in my career, but I cannot stomach this tripe. If you want to put out a revised edition of *Green Thumb*, you will have to do it yourself or have some specialist hack it out. Specialization, I am unalterably convinced, is a plague on all our houses.

Gideon
P.S. If you publish that book in any form, I will sue you.
P.P.S. Where are this quarter's royalties?

The chair in which Gideon sat was the only chair in the room. An ancient green wool rug covered the floor. The walls, except for two doors, a real window looking out upon the concrete and aluminum peaks and cliffs of a city, and the desk, were books from rug to ceiling, stacked, heaped, stuck in sideways, backwards, and upside down.

From behind the door on the opposite side of the room the clinking sounds started again. A man cursed. Gideon's eyebrows became a single thicket over his eyes.

Something crashed. In a blur of motion, Gideon was out of his chair. He flung open the door and revealed three men in a narrow, tiled closet. They were standing over the remains of what had been an excellent medicine cabinet.

Gideon thundered, "What in the name of Moloch do you think you're doing? Three men sent to do a boy's job, and you've been here all morning!"

A surly, dark-haired lavatorbot specialist second class said defensively, "This lavatorbot hasn't been repaired for so long it wouldn't work at all. When he tried to remove it, the thing slipped and fell."

Gideon asked dangerously, "Why didn't *you* remove it?"

The young man drew himself up proudly. "I am an electronic lavatorbot specialist. He"—the young man pointed—"is the mechanical lavatorbot specialist."

Muted violence was in his voice as Gideon said, "Did it ever occur to you that the lavatorbot was not a lavatorbot at all? It was a perfectly good machine chest, and you will procure me a new one immediately—and replacements for all the pharmaceuticals within." He pointed at the old-fashioned, white china commode in the corner. "That is what I wanted fixed—a simple, three-minute job an idiot child could perform."

"That is completely outside my specialty!"

Gideon pointed a pudgy finger at the third man, a tall, thin young man with red hair. "Why don't you fix it!"

The young man said indignantly, "I am a plumber, not an antiquarian. If you had a modern disposerbot, it would be a simple matter. That is an atrocity."

Gideon roared, "Keep my personal preferences out of this. Can you fix that thing?"

The plumber flinched. He said meekly, "What seems to be wrong with it?"

"It—won't—flush."

Gingerly the red-haired plumber twisted the handle on the water closet. Water gurgled into the bowl and swirled up dangerously close to the edge before it subsided. Slowly the level dropped. "Well," said the plumber. "Well. My suggestion is that you get rid of the whole affair. I can get a crew of men in a few days, rip this thing out, and put in a modern disposerbot—"

"Young man! I like this commode. I have become accustomed to it. I sometimes stand here for hours and flush it for recreation, just to listen to its long, withdrawing, melancholy roar." Gideon's pale eyes lighted on the plumber's open tool box. "What's that!"

"This?" The plumber picked up a rubber plunger on a stick. "This is known as a plumber's friend."

"No doubt the only one you have," Gregor said scathingly. "Use it!"

"This, sir," the plumber said icily, "is my specialist's badge. It is purely ornamental."

With a roar of rage, Gideon grabbed the plunger and jabbed it several times into the commode. The water surged down and out. "There! Now out! All of you!"

They fled before him, scrambling through the doorway and the room beyond, fumbling with the old-fashioned door into the hall. Gideon pursued them, the plumber's friend waving in one hand like a mace. Finally the lavatorbot specialist, electronic, got the door open, and they scattered in all directions down the hall.

With a triumphant swing of his arm, Gideon threw the plunger after them, narrowly missing a tall, gray-haired man whose hand was raised to knock on the door.

In a voice that was almost pleasant, Gideon said, "What in Beelzebub's name do you want?"

The man stared down the hall toward the spot where the plunger clung to the distant wall like a native spear and then looked back at Gideon with incredulous eyes. He blinked, and his expression sobered.

"I am Carl Vigran, psycho-specialist, administrative assistant, personnel, to the president of the University—"

"My time is worth money," Gideon snapped.

Vigran said simply, "Johnny Sundance has disappeared."

The lean, broad-shouldered young man had a face that was hard to forget. It was broad, flat, and copper-colored beneath a stiff, unruly mass of blue-black hair. The nose was prominent and aquiline, but the dark eyes were dull.

He lurched drunkenly as he stepped off the Fifth Avenue slidewalk. On the stationary pavement he caught himself and began walking aimlessly into the older part of the city.

People turned to look at him as he passed, but he saw none of them. He stopped, finally, and turned his face toward the building, his eyes closed, his forehead leaning against a black plate-glass window as if he were trying to cool it.

In a moment he reeled back and opened his eyes. Lavender words wriggled across the black glass. He squinted at them as if he were trying to read and couldn't. Then he turned and

*shouldered his way through the door. He stood, swaying, just
inside the entrance, staring blindly into the dim recesses of
the room.*

Gideon leaned back comfortably in his desk chair, studying
without pretense of manners the middle-aged man who stood
uncomfortably near the door. Vigran had taken good care of
himself; at sixty he was slim and vigorous. His face was thin
and sharp, stamped by the aristocracy of intelligence. He
looked younger than his prematurely gray hair suggested. Im-
peccably dressed in a gray one-piece business suit, he was a
brilliant man, a capable man, a specialist.

Gideon said calmly, "Johnny has disappeared. So?"

Vigran's poise shattered with the jerky movements of his
hands. "You haven't seen him?"

"Why should I?"

"You were his closest friend."

Gideon looked surprised. "Was I? Poor Johnny. What
about women?"

"When he's working on a problem, he hasn't time for anything else. None of them have seen him for months." Vigran
said urgently, "We've got to find him, McKenzie. If you can
help us in any way, if you can think of any place he might
have gone—"

Gideon's pale eyes studied Vigran's face. The psychospe-
cialist's lip was twitching. "What makes Johnny so much
more important than any of the others?"

Vigran said quickly, "What others?"

Gideon's voice was sharp. "Don't fence with me. The other
specialists who have disappeared, the other particle physi-
cists. You can bury them among the personals, but you can't
cover them up completely. How many have there been in the
last six months? Six? Seven?"

Vigran said unhappily, "Nine."

"How many have you found?"

"One. He—he came back."

Gideon said shrewdly, "Insane?"

Slowly Vigran nodded.

Thoughtfully Gideon placed the tips of his stubby fingers

together. "Quite an epidemic," he said cheerfully.

Vigran said, "They're all important. If we can solve one we'll have a clue to the others. But we need Johnny in particular. His recent work—his associates say it may be the most important research in the last fifty years. They can't decipher his notes. They jump over whole areas of development and proof to indecipherable conclusions. Interspersed are philosophical ramblings. Most uncharacteristic."

Gideon had tired of the conversation. He swung his chair toward the desk in a gesture of dismissal. "Sic your bloodhounds on him."

Vigran moved quickly to the desk, leaned over it to face Gideon. "They lost the trail, McKenzie. Like they did with the others. Their actions have not followed any anticipated pattern. Their movements have been random. McKenzie—you were Johnny's friend. For Johnny's sake!"

Gideon stared malevolently at Vigran. "I remember you. A year ago you refused me the use of the University library. Said a non-specialist could not make effective use of it."

"A misunderstanding!" Vigran gasped. "That will be corrected."

Gideon looked down at the palms of his pudgy hands. They were dirty. "How do you know he wants to come back?"

"He had everything he could have wanted. A free hand in his research, unrestricted grants to finance it, prestige, a large salary—why should he leave?" Vigran hesitated. "We're afraid of amnesia."

"Nine times? Amnesia is a myth. It was exploded many years ago. Why was he unhappy?"

Vigran said sharply, "He wasn't! He was at the top of his specialty in a profession that is universally admired. He was doing what he was best fitted for; he was using his talent to the fullest. He enjoyed his work. He had security, admiration, friends . . . What did he lack?"

"What indeed? You make it sound idyllic." Gideon said sharply, "But he ran away."

Vigran's hands fluttered ineffectually. "We don't know that he did. He just—disappeared."

A slow, pleased smile crept over Gideon's face. "You know

what's the matter with you? You're a specialist and you've
found a problem you can't solve. You're frustrated—just like
your bloodhounds. They must be thoroughly useless by
now." He chuckled happily. "Unless your problem is re-
solved, they'll be looking for you one of these days."

Vigran drew himself up stiffly. "You're forgetting yourself,
McKenzie."

"No, Vigran, you're forgetting that you came to me. You're
forgetting why you came to me. Not because I knew Johnny.
Your specialists could dig up more about Johnny than I could
possibly know. You came to me because I am the last of the
universal geniuses." He put his elbow on the desk, propped
his chin in his palm, and stared up complacently at Vigran.
He looked like a fat man's version of Rodin's Thinker.

Vigran gasped, "You're mad, McKenzie. But maybe you're
mad enough to find an answer. Everything else has failed."

Gideon was not insulted. "I'm interested. Two conditions.
First, I must have full access to your personnel and psycholo-
gical files, as well as Johnny's papers."

Vigran hesitated and then nodded.

"Two: when I find Johnny, he doesn't have to return unless
he wishes."

Vigran said indignantly, "What do you think the University is? A prison?"

"Yes," Gideon snarled. "A prison for minds."

*The servandroid stopped in front of the young man with
the copper-colored face and the dull, black eyes and said,
"You aren't well, sir. Shall I call a doctor?"*

*He brushed the thing aside and walked unsteadily into the
dim room, over the lavender carpet, toward a row of booths
against the far wall.*

*The place was almost deserted. It was quiet. The young
man staggered when he reached the booths and caught himself on a gray, plastic table. The schooner of beer on it sloshed
some of its contents onto the table. His eyes focused on the
glass. His dark hand reached out, lifted it to his lips. He
drained it.*

"What you think you're—" a hoarse voice began. A hand

grabbed the young man by the shoulder. The voice gentled.
"Say, you're sick."
Johnny Sundance slumped bonelessly into the booth.

The lavender words wriggling on the black plate-glass window spelled "Sam's Place." It was an ordinary neighborhood bar. Inside, it was gloomy, cool, and old-fashioned. The thick carpeting was lavender. The tables were gray plastic. The booths along the walls were upholstered in pink imitation leather. Female servandroids, their bodies sculptured perfection under their tiny, translucent uniforms, carried trays among the tables.

Carl Vigran hesitated blindly at the entrance and then stumbled down three steps before he saw Gideon. He made his way quickly to the booth. "Why did you want me to meet you here?"

Gideon raised to his lips an old-fashioned schooner of beer and sipped the foamy, yellow liquid gingerly. He wiped his mouth on the back of a hairy hand. "To find Johnny. This is where your bloodhounds lost the trail."

Vigram said impatiently, "I know that, but he isn't coming back. This place has been watched for days."

"Maybe," Gideon suggested slyly, "you were watching for the wrong person."

Vigran looked startled and pleased. "You've found him!"

"Sit down." Gideon waited until Vigran had slipped into the seat opposite. "No, I haven't found Johnny. Even a universal genius must have more than twenty-four hours. First I had to learn Johnny inside out. I had to be able to think like Johnny."

"Well?"

"Now I know Johnny like one of my own characters." Gideon drained his glass and summoned a servandroid. "Again," he said. "You see," he said to Vigran, "I am drinking beer, a drink I detest, because it was Johnny's favorite. Anything more potent was firewater, and the Indian has a notoriously weak stomach for alcohol, he used to say.

"Johnny and I met by accident. He had happened on a potboiler of mine called *Green Thumb*, written during a brief period of insanity when I was under the spell of modern education. He wrote to me, asking where he should continue his work on quantum physics. He was ten at the time.

"I had come to my senses. I tried to discourage him, but he persisted. I turned his letter over to the University, and you recruited him, bending the NCAA regulations somewhat in the process."

Vigran leaned toward Gideon. He said abruptly, "That's better forgotten."

"Later Johnny insisted on coming around and thanking me for my help. Frequently. He had an engagingly inquisitive mind, and my broad range of interests fascinated him. I tried to expand his scope, but he was a specialist and satisfied to be that and nothing more."

The servandroid brought back Gideon's glass. He patted her familiarly as she bent over the table.

Vigran exploded. "That's an android!"

Gideon winked expressively. "You know that, and I know that. But does she know that? Ah, well." He shrugged. "At first I suspected women, but Johnny has had the normal sexual experiences for his maturation group, including some with older women infatuated by his reputation. Lately he became more fastidious. He has led, it appears, a full, satisfying life."

Vigran said, "I told you that much. But why did he disappear?" His lip jerked. It was getting worse.

"For the same reason the others disappeared."

Vigran's hand began to pound on the table. He didn't notice. "Why? Do you have a theory?"

Gideon leaned back contemptuously. "Many. Theories are cheap. For instance, they may have been kidnapped by extraterrestrials."

Vigran made a disgusted face.

"All right," Gideon said mildly, "scratch theory number one. Number two: when men get too intelligent they learn something that the rest of us are too stupid to see, that makes further effort futile.

"Number three: modern education is forced growth. The tendency of many child prodigies to fail in later life is an infantile rebellion against authority.

"Theory number four: thinking is a disease. Intelligence, like size, adaptability, prolificness, speed, and so forth, is an evolutionary experiment. All of them are survival characteristics, and all of them carry within themselves the seeds of their own destruction.

"The trouble with intelligence is that it sees problems and seeks answers. The one thing intelligence must have which it cannot manipulate like its environment is understanding. And ultimate understanding is impossible. Result: madness or its equivalent, the rejection of intelligence."

Vigran's expression had progressed from incredulity to contempt. "Which one do you prefer?" he asked sarcastically.

Gideon shrugged his plump shoulders. "All of them. None of them. I always wait for the proof of experimental evidence. Which we are about to get. See that man?"

Vigran looked up. Passing them was a short, thick young man with long, untrimmed blond hair and a pale, scowling face. He glanced suspiciously at everyone he passed. In his hand he had a round, yellow, plastic container. He started up the steps toward the entrance.

Vigran whispered. "That isn't Johnny!"

With great disgust, Gideon said, "Who said it was? He will lead us to Johnny."

It was early morning when they came out. The streets were deserted. There was no one to notice a tall, black-haired, copper-skinned man and the short, thick blond who supported him as they walked.

Johnny reeled and almost fell. The blond caught him, held him up. "Just a little farther, Johnny. Then we'll be home."

"Home?" Johnny said. He began to laugh. "Home sweet home. Home is where the heart is. Home is the sailor, home from the sea, and the hunter home from the hill." The laughter broke into a sob.

"Shhhh, Johnny! Here we are." Carefully the blond young man led Johnny down a short flight of steps and put out a hand against the door plate. The door swung open. Warm, humid air came out to meet them. It was thick with the odor

of green, growing things.

As soon as the young man was gone, Gideon moved swiftly toward the door. A servandroid stepped quickly into his path and said pleasantly, "Your bill, sir?"

Gideon jerked a thumb at Vigran. "He'll pay."

When Vigran had caught up with Gideon, the lumpy man was gazing intently into a shop window. It featured a display of stretch shoes. There were all about size five. The sign on the window said, "This is your size."

"You're mad!" Vigran panted.

"Shhhh! He's gone into the seed shop across the street."

The short, thick man came out of the store, glancing both ways. He did not notice Gideon or Vigran, whom Gideon had swung around to face the shop window.

"Now," Gideon said. He turned and walked casually down the street. The stocky man was just turning the corner ahead. Now he had two containers in his hand. "Ah!" Gideon said.

Vigran trotted to keep up with Gideon. "That fellow can't have anything to do with Johnny. He's obviously an unspecialized laborer."

"Hah!" Gideon said. They turned the corner. Their quarry was disappearing into the basement entrance of a decrepit, green-tinted concrete slab apartment building. "I see now why you couldn't possibly find Johnny. It's because of the very nature of specialization."

Vigran said crisply, "Nonsense! I don't know what you're doing, but I know this much: without specialization our society would have disintegrated long ago."

Gideon breathed noisily through his putty nose. "Specialists are tame animals. They are trained to do one thing well. But what happens when they meet totally unforeseen conditions? They fail. They cannot cope, because that is the function of the wild, unspecialized animal. You couldn't find Johnny because his disappearance was unpredictable.

"Every science that deals with man ignores everything except what it deals with. Medicine deals with the physical man, economics with that simplification known as Economic Man, psychiatry with a fictitious creature in whom it would have no interest if he were 'normal,' and one branch of psychology with I.Q. Man, whose only significant aspect is his ability to solve puzzles.

"Literature is the only thing that deals with the whole complex phenomenon at once. If it were to cease to exist, whatever is not considered by one or another of the sciences would no longer be considered at all and would perhaps vanish completely."

Skepticism battled hope across Vigran's face. "Then he's in there?"

"We shall see." Gideon waddled heavily down the concrete steps. "Carl Vigran to see Johnny Sundance," he said to the red door.

The door cleared its throat rustily. "This is the residence of Otto Haber. There is no one here named Johnny Sundance."

"Announce me," Gideon said sharply. "Carl Vigran."

Vigran asked sharply, "Why don't you use your own name?"

"He's afraid of me." The door stood silent and unmoved. "Come, Otto," Gideon muttered. "We are waiting."

Vigran said, "What makes you think he's here?"

Gideon said, "Johnny was fleeing. He was trying to escape. He needed something he had not had for fourteen years—emotional security."

Vigran said in a pained voice, "You're talking my specialty. That isn't done—not by a layman."

"I'm talking about something you've forgotten: love. The kind that asks nothing but the chance to love. The kind that makes no demands, that incurs no responsibilities. Johnny stumbled into Sam's Place—and met Otto."

Vigran looked startled. "What are you trying to imply?"

Gideon turned his massive head so that his pale blue eyes looked straight and hard at Vigran. "Nothing. I am telling you what happened. If you want to make inferences, I can assure you that they are wrong. No one noticed Johnny when he left Sam's Place because he came in alone and left with Otto. No one saw him on the street because it was very late, and your bloodhounds were looking for one man, not two. And here Johnny has been ever since."

Gideon turned back to the door and began to bang on it with his fist.

"Please!" said the doorbot in a shocked voice. "Sir!"

Vigran said, "All right, then, how did you find him?"

"I checked the central retail food billings. In this neighborhood, only one person's bill has increased in the last few days without reason. Otto Haber's." A furtive note of doubt crept into Gideon's voice. "Oddly enough, though, only by about one-third."

Disgustedly Vigran said, "Guesswork! I should have known better than to follow a fool on a fool's errand." He took a step toward the street.

The door opened a crack. The stocky young man's blond, suspicious face peered out. "What you want?" he asked hoarsely.

"We've come to see Johnny," Gideon said quietly.

"Never heard of him. Ain't nobody here but me." He tried to slam the door, but Gideon was leaning against it. "Get out of here!"

"When we see Johnny," Gideon said.

Vigran tugged at Gideon's sleeve. "Come on, McKenzie. Don't get us both into trouble."

Otto paid no attention to Vigran. His hard eyes were fixed on Gideon. "You got a warrant says you can break in a man's home?"

Gideon shook his head. "No warrant. We can get one if we have to. But if we get a warrant you'll lose Johnny for sure. All we want to do is see him, and we'll leave. If Johnny doesn't want to come, this man promises to leave him alone."

Otto shifted his glaring eyes to Vigran and back again to Gideon. "Who's he?"

"Administrative assistant to the president at the University. Where Johnny was. He wants Johnny back. Let us in now and that will be the end of it."

Unexpectedly the door swung open. "All right," Otto snarled. "See him and get out!"

Otto carried the packages into the bedroom, for once not stopping to look at his flowers or the tank farm. His face was eager as he handed Johnny the plastic container. "Here, Johnny. Here's your beer."

The copper-faced young man lying on the rumpled bed, his black eyes staring blindly at the ceiling with its intricate network of fine cracks, slowly sat up. He took the container and tore off the strip that sealed the top. He raised it to his thin lips and then spat a mouthful on the floor beside the bed. "It's warm," he said flatly. "You stopped somewhere."

"Honest, Johnny," Otto said. "Just long enough to get some bug spray. It must have been warm when they sold it to me. I'll take it back, Johnny. You want I should take it back?"

"No. I don't want it anyway." Johnny laid down again and looked at the mottled wall.

Hopefully Otto said, "I'm gonna make some stew tonight. I got me some real beef bouillon cubes. I'll get me some potatoes and carrots and cabbage fresh from the farm—Johnny, is there something wrong?"

"Anybody follow you?"

"No, Johnny. I was careful like you said."

"Then why is somebody at the door?"

Otto raised his head and listened. He could hear it now, the cracked voice of the doorbot saying, "Carl Vigran for Johnny Sundance."

Otto said, "I won't go. They got no business here. They'll think nobody's home. They'll go away."

Contemptuously Johnny said, "They saw you come in. Answer the door."

"Johnny, what are you gonna do?"

"Don't let Vigran in. He'll need a warrant. He's a fool. He'll go away, but he'll be back. As soon as he goes away, I'll leave."

Slowly Otto said, "Where would you go, Johnny? What would you do?"

"Who cares? Now answer the door, stupid!"

Otto said softly, "Don't leave me, Johnny."

There was a short entrance hall lined on either side with a long box filled with flowers. Their colors were brilliant under the sunlamps beaming down warmly from the ceiling: bright

yellow, scarlet, gentian blue, purple, violet, emerald . . . The
air was warm and steamy and filled with the odor of green
things growing and the mingled scent of many flowers.

Otto had an aerosol spray in one hand. He held it as if it
were a bomb he was prepared to throw at any moment.

Gideon glanced sharply at the flowers and then led Vigran
down the hall over the pitted green plastic tile. The hall
opened into a small living room. The room was dim, but the
odor of vegetation was even stronger. The room was made
even smaller by a wide, flat tank that covered two-thirds of
the floor. There were vegetables growing in it—potatoes, carrots, beets, tomatoes, green beans, corn—their roots floating
in a nutrient solution. Somewhere a pump gurgled quietly. It
was the only sound in the room.

Gideon's eyes brightened. "Ah. Fresh food!"

Otto sneered. "He's in there!" He pointed to a doorway.

Gideon stopped just inside the next room. It was even
smaller than the living room. There was space for a bed, a
marred black table, and two rickety chairs. Curtains closed
off an alcove. Gideon guessed that it was a cooking area. The
room was sour and dirty.

Johnny was propped up in the bed, the covers wrinkled and
gray around him. Beside him was a plastic container of beer.
His broad, flat face was turned toward the doorway. He
looked at Gideon for a moment with obsidian eyes and then
turned his head toward the wall. The room was silent.

"These men," Otto said softly. "They come to see you,
Johnny. You know them?"

Johnny didn't move.

Vigran edged into the room and took it in with one horrified glance. "Johnny! What are you doing here? Why did
you run away? What—?"

Gideon said flatly, "Shut up!" He walked over to one of the
chairs and drew it up to the bed. Gingerly he eased his massive body onto it, listening to it creak beneath him. When he
was sure it would not collapse beneath him, he leaned forward.

He said gently, "Johnny! We aren't going to stay long. We
aren't going to take you away unless you want to come. We

just want to talk for a moment."

Johnny stared at the wall. Finally, without turning, he said tonelessly, "What are you doing here?"

"Vigran asked me to help."

"Why did you?"

"It was the only way I could be sure he wouldn't cart you off if he did find you. He promised to leave you alone if you decide to stay."

Indignantly Vigran said, "McKenzie!"

"Shut up!" Gideon said wearily.

Johnny said, "How did you find me?"

"Chance," Gideon said.

A slow tremor ran over Johnny's lean body. "No. You thought it all out. You knew. Why don't you leave me alone?"

"We will, Johnny," Gideon said. "In just a moment. I know why you ran away."

Johnny turned his head to look at Gideon. His black eyes were fierce and hawklike. "Do you? Do you really? Do you know what it is to realize that you have wasted your life, that everything you have tried to do is futile, that nothing has any meaning?"

Gideon said, "Yes."

Johnny said violently, "Chance rules the universe. Man is only a minute flyspeck in the cosmos, tossed here and there by the Brownian Movement of fate. He's still a mindless blob of protoplasm.

"I know now what killed my parents. Not an airplane. Chance. Chance brought me to the University. Chance drove me away."

Vigran whispered to Gideon, "I'll get help."

Gideon didn't look away from Johnny. "Stay where you are! He isn't crazy."

Coldly Johnny said, "No. I'm sane. Too sane. Too sane for my own good."

"Come back, Johnny," Vigran pleaded. "If there was anything wrong with the way we treated you, if—" He looked at Johnny's eyes and stopped.

Gideon said, "He doesn't understand, Johnny. I think

maybe you owe him an explanation. Other men have disappeared. It's driving him insane."

"Let him read my notes. It's all there."

Otto had been looking at Johnny without understanding. Now he said, "You want I should throw them out, Johnny?" Vigran turned on him furiously. "You, Haber! You know what you've got here in this rat's nest? The finest mind of our generation. He's got more than fifty thousand dollars in the bank, and he's lying here in rags and filth."

Otto's puzzled eyes turned back toward Johnny. "Is that right, Johnny? You got all that money?"

Johnny shrugged. "What good is it?"

"You could go back to that?"

"I'm never going back."

Otto took a step toward the bed. "I been keeping you, buying you beer. And you got fifty thousand. You're no good, Johnny! I don't like you." His voice was climbing toward a scream. "Get out!" He hit Johnny across the face with the back of his hand. "Get out!"

The most important single gift of science to civilization was freedom from superstition: the idea that order, not caprice, governs the world, that man was capable of understanding it Beginning with Newton's discovery of the universal sway of the law of gravitation, man felt himself to be in a congenial universe; all things were subject to universal laws.

But that conviction arose from the narrowness of his horizons. When he extended his range he found that nature was neither understandable nor subject to law. For this we may thank Planck, Einstein, Bohr, and Heisenberg.

Heisenberg's uncertainty principle set an unsuspected limit on the accuracy with which we can describe physical situations. If we measure one quality accurately we can't do the same for another. Perfect accuracy in the measurement of the position of an electron denies us any measurement at all of its velocity. Therefore an electron can't have both position and velocity.

A physical concept has meaning to the physicist only in terms of some sort of measurement. A body has position only in so far as its position can be measured. If it can't be measured, the concept is meaningless—a position of the body doesn't exist. By choosing whether we shall measure position or velocity, we determine which of those qualities the electron has. The physical properties of an electron are not inherent; they involve the choice of the observer.

The law of cause and effect is invalid; it gives only an approximation (just as quantum mechanics gives its answers only in statistical probability). Events are not causally connected; the concept of cause has no meaning.

Whenever we observe something, our sensory equipment reacts on the object observed, and that interaction can't be reduced below a minimum. When the minimum interaction is taking place, the object can't be observed; we can't measure with an instrument as coarse as the thing we are trying to analyze.

The physicist has come to the end of his domain. He has reached the point where knowledge must stop because of the nature of knowledge itself. Beyond this point, meaning ceases. We do not live in a world of reason, understandable by the intellect of man. As we penetrate deeper, the very law of cause and effect which we had thought to be a formula to which we could force God himself to subscribe, ceases to have meaning.

(Excerpt from the notebooks of Johnny Sundance)

Johnny looked at Otto with eyes that were suddenly warm with knowledge. While his cheek slowly grew a darker red, he said gently, "Don't be a fool, Otto. You can't drive me away." He looked at Vigran. "I don't think I can ever forgive you."

Gideon said, "He's desperate. He's lost."

"There's no way of predicting photon movements," Johnny threw at Vigran. "No way at all. They're governed by chance."

Vigran looked bewildered and afraid. "That doesn't make sense. That's no reason to—"

Gideon said ironically, "It isn't your specialty. The function of intelligence is to solve problems. What if it finds a problem for which there can be no solution? It protects itself by going mad or denying its own existence. Johnny is a specialist, and his specialty has led him into a blind alley where the only way to go is out the way he came in."

Johnny repeated, "Chance rules the universe."

"That's—that's nothing but superstition."

Gideon said, "Science giveth and science taketh away."

"Get this," Johnny said. "This is the last time I'll say it, the last time I'll think about it. You're trying to determine the position and velocity of an electron. In order for it to be seen, a photon must strike it and be reflected into your detection instrument, but the very act of striking deflects the electron so that it isn't where it was or it isn't going with the velocity it had.

"Make two slits. Reflect a photon so that it may enter either one. Which does it enter? Sometimes one, sometimes the other. And you can't ever be sure which!"

Vigran shook his head desperately. "But that all takes place at the level of the electron. It doesn't affect us."

Gideon said, "Compton suggested an experiment in which a ray of light is diffracted through two slits so that it may enter either of two photoelectric cells. Through one it explodes a stick of dynamite; through the other it throws a switch which prevents the dynamite from exploding. What determines whether the dynamite explodes? Chance."

Johnny said quickly, "In the same way the nervous system of a living organism acts as an amplifier, so that its actions depend on events on so small a scale that they are subject to Heisenberg Uncertainty. A neuron fires or does not fire because at a lower level an electron goes one way or another."

Vigran looked back and forth between them. "But then it's an old idea. You already knew this, Johnny. Why should it bother you now?"

Johnny shivered. "I accepted it intellectually. Now I know it. It's no use trying to understand the universe. Intelligence is worthless. The universe is governed by pure chance." With a finality that seemed beyond argument, Johnny turned his head once more to the wall. "Now go away."

Vigran began, "But—"

Otto turned on Vigran savagely as if he was hoping for

resistance. "You heard him. Get out!"

"Just a moment," Gideon said quietly. "I'd like to talk to you a moment, Otto. How would you like a job?"

Johnny turned his head to look back at Gideon suspiciously. Otto's eyes narrowed. "What kind of job?"

"Doing what you're doing here. Growing things. Only all the time and with more equipment."

"Where?" Otto said hoarsely.

"At the University."

"McKenzie—" Vigran exclaimed.

"Shut up, Vigran! What do you say, Otto?"

"What do they want food for?" Otto asked sullenly.

"Not food, Otto—knowledge."

"See here, McKenzie!" Vigran broke in. "We can't hire him. He's a layman. He doesn't have a specialty or a degree—"

Gideon turned on him fiercely. "You're interested in the green thumb phenomenon. Talent isn't all intellectual. How did he do that?" He jerked his thumb toward the tank filled with flourishing vegetation."

Vigran spluttered, "Why he just—He knows—"

"A layman? Without a specialty or a degree? He doesn't know anything. He's got a green thumb. Why?"

"Maybe," Vigran muttered. "Maybe."

Gideon turned back to Otto. "What do you say, Otto? It means two or three times what you're making now. It means a chance to do what you like to do. Grow things. And find out why they grow for you."

Johnny said fiercely, "Don't do it, Otto! They'll tear you apart!"

Otto frowned. "What about Johnny?"

"He can live with you at the University until he decides what he wants to do."

Johnny said, "It's just a trick, Otto!"

"I don't go without Johnny."

"Let me talk to him," Gideon said. "For the last time. Go talk to Dr. Vigran about the job."

Otto hesitated for a moment and then with a long look at Johnny left the room. The little room was silent for a long time while Gideon and Johnny looked at each other. "Why are you doing this to me?" Johnny asked. Gideon said, "I know what you're going through." Violently Johnny said, "You! What do you know?" "I went through it myself. These others—they can't understand what it is to stake their lives on an idea—and feel the idea vanish beneath them. You're floundering, Johnny, trying to find solid ground. Don't do yourself irreparable damage in the process."

"You're lying to me."

Gideon took a deep breath. For a moment he looked not like a lumpy old man but a hero. "Look at me, Johnny! Why do you think I'm a fat buffoon wasting my talent on potboilers. Why do I punish myself and the world, lashing out at everyone who comes within tongue's range? Because I lived too long with fear and despair."

Johnny said hopelessly, "There isn't any solid ground."

"Think of this. If cause and effect is overthrown, so is predestination. Free will is given back to Man. He can choose without the inner certainty that the choice was made for him by an inexorable pattern fixed in the instant of the explosion of the primordial giant atom. You're free, Johnny. You can be whatever you want to be—except God."

Johnny laughed, but his voice broke in the middle. "Who wants to be God—that must be a lousy job. But what else is there to be?"

"A man. A suffering, erring, loving man. A free man. God is inextricably bound by his own omniscience. Only man is free."

"But what is there to do?"

"Perhaps there are other routes besides intelligence, other ways to control chance. Ask Otto how he does it; ask him in a way he can answer, as you would ask a question of nature. Other people have similar talents. Find out how they work, and perhaps you can make another assault on the citadel of ultimate knowledge."

Johnny stretched his arms out wide and sat up on the edge of the bed. Suddenly he looked very young. "Perhaps," he said. "I'll—I'll think about it."

Gideon said gently, "Yes, Johnny. You think about it."

In the next room, Gideon said, "Go in with Johnny, Otto. I think he would like to talk to you."

Vigran whispered, "Well? Will he come back?"

Gideon nodded wearily. "Yes. He'll come back." His pale eyes moved slowly around the room. He stared thoughtfully at the hydroponic tank.

"What about the others?"

Gideon spun around angrily. "That's your responsibility! I do not like to play God." His voice dropped. "I do not like it at all."

7. The Power And The Glory

THE SUN SANK slowly below the purple hills. The tattered clouds that streamed up the western sky were orange, red, and violet banners flying above a tragic army marching beyond the horizon to some final glory.

They watched it from inside the room, the man and his visitor. The window that framed the scene was the only place in the room, except the door, that had not been submerged in a tide of books. They had mounted the walls and toppled into corners and reached tooled-leather fingers across the floor.

The visitor stood in front of the window, his stocky figure silhouetted against the light. He was a little blurred around the edges, like an afterimage that is beginning to fade. But he was solid enough.

The room was silent. But the silence was rippled with words that had been spoken—the way a still pond remembers the pebbles tossed into it.

As the colors faded in the west, a husky voice spoke out of the silence and out of the darkness that clasped one corner of the room, revealing only the arm of a tapestry-covered chair, a hand that rested motionless upon it and a foot stuck out stiffly onto a stool, the thin sole touched by a single orange ray of sun.

"How will it end?" the voice asked.

The answer came over the visitor's shoulder in cultured resonant words with a hint of accent like those of a foreigner who has learned to speak the language better than the natives.

"In fire, in ice, with a bang, with a whimper, by cosmic accident, by man's own will and hand. What does it matter?"

"I would know."

"That is the most persistent trait.of intelligence."

"You will not tell me?"

"Perhaps I do not know. Perhaps I cannot say. We are not gods, you know."

"What are you, then?"

"Scientists, experimenters. In your language those words might describe us best."

"And we are your experiment."

The visitor turned around. His face, too, was shadowed.

"Yes."

"And now the experiment is over."

"We have found out what we wished to know. We clean the test tube, sterilize the equipment. You should understand."

"Understand? I should not even believe—and yet I do. Without knowing why."

"All your life has been preparation for this moment. You cannot help but believe. But you also must understand."

"Intellectually I do. Emotionally I cannot accept the statement that this experiment has achieved its purpose—that man cannot achieve more."

"It is not men, you understand, but the experiment. Men have had millions of years, hundreds of thousands of generations, thousands of civilizations. What men can do further is repetition. And yet—"

"Do you give me hope?" the husky voice asked.

"There is no hope. There is only this odd contradiction in man that you mention, this tension between his intelligence and his animal instincts. He calls it emotion. The curious interplay between your reason and instincts has kept us fascinated long past the experiment's planned duration. But there are many more odd facets to the universe that we would explore and this small complication has preoccupied us too long. We can deal with the curious fact of man in ways that are not so complex—nor so expensive."

"Leave us. Let us live out our destiny."

"We are your destiny. You exist only as an experiment. Does the scientist leave his laboratory to build another when one experiment is completed? Neither do we. And although this laboratory—the very concept of which staggers your imagination—is only one among many, we do not waste. To us waste is unimaginable."

"If you have no love for what you have created—have you no pity?"

"None."

"No feeling?"

"None. We are rational beings. Our only motivation is the search for knowledge. Perhaps once—so far back in the mists of our beginning that even we have forgotten—we had that confusion of intellect that you call feeling. If so, it has been lost irretrievably. We can no more keep from doing the rational than you can stop breathing. On the other hand, you have evolved recently and rapidly. You are an accretion of characteristics, some of them incompatible."

The man said nothing.

"We had speculated that intelligence is the superior and dominant characteristic," the visitor continued. "But we found that among men this is true only occasionally. These men you call monsters. We find them dull. But you confused and emotional ones have fascinated us beyond your allotted span."

"You are the monsters."

"You would consider us so. And yet we do nothing that is not rational, whereas you use your intelligence largely to rationalize the crimes you commit against your fellows."

"We create," said the man.

The visitor stepped forward. His shoes and trousered legs looked ordinary in the light cast from a distant corner by a floor lamp. His shoulders and face still were in darkness.

"Yes, you create—far beyond your predictable powers. Insanely, without plan or reason. Your creation is a magnificent waste; we cannot understand it because we cannot waste. We do not have what you call art or music or literature. We do not understand what you call beauty or what you call ugliness —except in theory."

"Then man has something to offer—something you do not have. He can complement your rational existence with his irrational creativity. With his assistance there is nothing you cannot do, no goals to which you cannot aspire."

"We do not wish to do anything. We aspire to nothing except to knowledge. And that we seek in our own rational ways —which the addition of emotion would only muddle. And now, of course, man seeks to move beyond this test tube in which the human experiment began and to infest and to destroy other experiments. To allow you to do so would not be rational. Your defense of mankind is futile. Man cannot be saved. He is doomed."

The man in the shadows sighed. After a moment he said, "You let slip the fact that there are other ways to deal with the fact of man."

"I let nothing slip. We make no mistakes."

"What are these ways? Would you try to understand us intellectually? Will you run us through your computers until we make sense?"

"That is not possible. But ever since the end of the experiment has been obvious—for the last three millennia—we have chosen the most creative among you. They have been— there is not quite the word in your language to describe it— translated into another existence. We have chosen religious innovators, military leaders, political geniuses, philosophers, artists, writers, composers, scientists—"

"Christ and Mohammed?"

"And Gautama Siddhartha."

"Machiavelli?"

"And Solon and Jefferson."

"Plato and Aristotle?"

"And Kant and Nietzsche."

"Michelangelo?"

"And Praxiteles and Picasso."

"Shakespeare?"

"And Homer and Hemingway."

"Bach and Beethoven?"

"Brahms and Berlioz."

"Archimedes?"

"Galileo and Newton and Einstein. There are thousands more and thousands whose names you never heard—all of them creators. And that is why I am here tonight."

"I wondered. I am none of these. I have never created anything."

"You are one of them," the visitor said. "The fact that you have not exercised your creativity yet is incidental. We may not have it ourselves—we may not understand it—but we have learned to recognize creativity and its signs. In the relative eternity to come you will have time to be creative."

"Me. Among them?"

"You are one of them—of equal stature. You can be one of them for long ages, interacting with them, learning from them as they will learn from you and we from all—in a way that you have only imagined here among your books."

"Incredible—"

"In your terms—yes."

"My dreams. Heaven."

"So we understand."

"If I were a superstitious man of another age, I would think you an emissary of the devil come to tempt me."

"We are all the devil and all the god you imagine—both and neither. In another age we spoke in their language and in their frame of reference, as we speak to you in yours."

"In what way would existence continue?"

The man had leaned forward until his upper body, clothed in a gray sweater, was in the light, although his face still was in the shadows.

"In a way much like what you experience now, with certain measures taken to delay your mortality."

"And where would it continue?"

"In a place removed from here but one you would find pleasant, stocked with all the things you enjoy—the food, the drink, the books, the music and the art—and the people and the talk and the ideas and the time to contemplate and to create."

"Stop. You describe heaven."

"So you would consider it."

"You know me well."

"What we can know we know well."

The silence returned while the man sank back in his chair

and the visitor looked back toward the west where the sunset had faded and the twilight had darkened into night. The evening star gleamed brilliantly alone above the hills.

Finally the man spoke again. "What of my wife?"

The visitor turned back to the room. "The person who let me in—but only when I insisted? Who called you a fool?"

"Yes."

"You do not find her attractive."

"I did once."

"You do not love her."

"Once I did."

"She is not exceptional. We cannot save her. In any case, you will not lack for feminine companionship of a more congenial sort in the place where you are going."

The man laughed.

"Not only heaven but paradise."

"So you will consider it."

"I believe, after all, that you are an emissary of the devil—you know so well how to tempt a man."

"We are rational."

"And you want to understand the irrational. What about the rest of humanity?"

"A few, like you, we will save. The rest will be destroyed. They are worthless, redundant. Even you will admit this."

"In my more rational moments—perhaps I would. But why do you come to me this way and explain these things to me? If I accepted them as reality—as more than the strange ravings of a madman or the stranger imaginings of my own mind—why should you not merely take me away when you destroy the rest?"

"Perhaps your understanding is a condition of the translation. Perhaps it is part of the experiment. Perhaps it is both."

"Or neither. What if I should refuse?"

The visitor stopped in the act of speaking. For the first time he appeared uncertain. He stepped forward. He wore an ordinary blue jacket.

"Why should you? Why should you throw away what you desire most?"

"Would you take me anyway?"

The man leaned forward into the light. He was in his middle years—still vigorous but no longer young.

"No. It would do you no good to refuse, however. You would be throwing away your chances of eternity and the satisfactions of creation in a foolish gesture. You cannot save mankind."

"I cannot be a party to its destruction either. If the others before me agreed to your proposal—perhaps they did not have to contemplate the imminent obliteration of the rest."

The visitor stepped forward fully into the light. He had an ordinary face. Now it seemed disturbed.

"You would refuse?"

"Yes. I refuse."

"But why? What do you gain? What can you hope to achieve?"

"Perhaps I refuse the essential conditions of your offer. Perhaps by this act I refuse to join those who would profit from the sufferings they inflict on those capable of understanding the nature of their plight. Perhaps I refuse to profit personally from an act which destroys my race. Perhaps I choose to demonstrate to you in this conclusive fashion that you do not understand man at all, that all the other experiments you might perform are meaningless beside this one, that you wipe it out not because it is finished but because you cannot understand it."

"You are willing to risk so much?"

"All."

"You will not change your mind?"

"I will not."

"So I see."

"Thank you for your offer. It was enticing—but I must regretfully decline. I think you can find the way out."

The man in the book-cluttered room sat quietly in his chair for a long time after his visitor had left. Then he rose, walked to a desk in the corner, took paper from it and a pen and began to write.

In the street outside, the visitor looked toward the house he had just left and then toward the dark hills where the evening star now had set and Orion was sinking. He stood there for a long time before he faded like an afterimage and was gone.

8. *The Listeners*

"Is there anybody there?" said the Traveler,
Knocking on the moonlit door. . . .

THE VOICES BABBLED.

MacDonald heard them and knew that there was meaning in them, that they were trying to communicate and that he could understand them and respond to them if he could only concentrate on what they were saying, but he couldn't bring himself to make the effort. He tried again.

"Back behind everything, lurking like a silent shadow behind the closed door, is the question we can never answer except positively: Is there anybody there?"

That was Bob Adams, eternally the devil's advocate, looking querulously at the others around the conference table. His round face was sweating, although the mahogany-paneled room was cool.

Saunders puffed hard on his pipe. "But that's true of all science. The image of the scientist eliminating all negative possibilities is ridiculous. Can't be done. So he goes ahead on faith and statistical probability."

MacDonald watched the smoke rise above Saunders's head in clouds and wisps until it wavered in the draft from the air duct, thinned out, disappeared. He could not see it, but the odor reached his nostrils. It was an aromatic blend easily distinguishable from the flatter smell of cigarettes being smoked by Adams and some of the others.

Wasn't this their task? MacDonald wondered. To detect the thin smoke of life that drifts through the universe, to separate one trace from another, molecule by molecule, and then force them to reverse their entropic paths into their ordered and meaningful original form.

All the king's horses, and all the king's men. . . . Life itself is impossible, he thought, but men exist by reversing en-
tropy.

Down the long table cluttered with overflowing ash trays
and coffee cups and doodled scratch pads Olsen said, "We
always knew it would be a long search. Not years but centuries. The computers must have sufficient data, and that
means bits of information approximating the number of
molecules in the universe. Let's not chicken out now.

> *"If seven maids with seven mops*
> *Swept it for half a year,*
> *Do you suppose," the Walrus said,*
> *"That they could get it clear?"*

". . . ridiculous," someone was saying, and then Adams
broke in, "It's easy for you to talk about centuries when
you've been here only three years. Wait until you've been at
it for ten years, like I have. Or Mac here who has been on the
Project for twenty years and head of it for fifteen."

"What's the use of arguing about something we can't know
anything about?" Sonnenborn said reasonably. "We have to
base our position on probabilities. Shklovskii and Sagan estimated that there are more than one thousand million habi-
table planets in our galaxy alone. Von Hoerner estimated that
one in three million have advanced societies in orbit around
them; Sagan said one in one hundred thousand. Either way
it's good odds that there's somebody there—three hundred or
ten thousand in our segment of the universe. Our job is to listen in the right place or in the right way or understand what
we hear."

Adams turned to MacDonald. "What do you say, Mac?"

"I say these basic discussions are good for us," MacDonald
said mildly, "and we need to keep reminding ourselves what
it is we're doing, or we'll get swallowed in a quicksand of
data. I also say that it's time now to get down to the business
at hand—what observations do we make tonight and the rest
of the week before our next staff meeting?"

Saunders began, "I think we should make a methodical
sweep of the entire galactic lens, listening on all wave-

lengths—"
"We've done that a hundred times," said Sonnenborn.
"Not with my new filter—"
"Tau Ceti still is the most likely," said Olsen. "Let's really
give it a hearing—"
MacDonald heard Adams grumbling, half to himself, "If
there is anybody, and they are trying to communicate, some
amateur is going to pick it up on his ham set, decipher it on
his James Bond coderule, and leave us sitting here on one
hundred million dollars of equipment with egg all over our
faces—"
"And don't forget," MacDonald said, "tomorrow is Saturday night and Maria and I will be expecting you all at our
place at eight for the customary beer and bull. Those who
have more to say can save it for them."
MacDonald did not feel as jovial as he tried to sound. He
did not know whether he could stand another Saturday night
session of drink and discussion and dissension about the Project. This was one of his low periods when everything
seemed to pile up on top of him, and he could not get out
from under, or tell anybody how he felt. No matter how he
felt, the Saturday nights were good for the morale of the
others.

> *Pues no es posible que esté continuo el arco armado*
> *ni la condición y flaqueza humana se pueda sus-*
> *tenar sin alguna lícita recreación*

Within the Project, morale was always a problem. Besides,
it was good for Maria. She did not get out enough. She needed to see people. And then. . . .
And then maybe Adams was right. Maybe nobody was
there. Maybe nobody was sending signals because there was
nobody to send signals. Maybe man was all alone in the universe. Alone with God. Or alone with himself, whichever was
worse.
Maybe all the money was being wasted, and the effort, and
the preparation—all the intelligence and education and ideas
being drained away into an endlessly empty cavern.

> *Habe nun, ach! Philosophie,*
> *Juristerei and Medizin,*
> *Und leider auch Theologie*

Durchaus studiert, mit heissem Bemühn.
Da steh' ich nun, ich armer Tor!
Und bin so klug als wie zuvor;
Heisse Magister, heisse Doktor gar,
Und ziehe schon an die zehen Jahr
Herauf, herab und quer und krumm
Meine Schüler an der Nase herum—
Und sehe, dass wir nichts wissen können!

Poor fool. Why me? MacDonald thought. Could not some other lead them better, not by the nose but by his real wisdom? Perhaps all he was good for was the Saturday night parties. Perhaps it was time for a change.

He shook himself. It was the endless waiting that wore him down, the waiting for something that did not happen, and the Congressional hearings were coming up again. What could he say that he had not said before? How could he justify a project that already had gone on for nearly fifty years without results and might go on for centuries more?

"Gentlemen," he said briskly, "to our listening posts."

By the time he had settled himself at his disordered desk, Lily was standing beside him.

"Here's last night's computer analysis," she said, putting down in front of him a thin folder. "Reynolds says there's nothing there, but you always want to see it anyway. Here's the transcription of last year's Congressional hearings." A thick binder went on top of the folder. "The correspondence and the actual appropriation measure are in another file if you want them."

Mac Donald shook his head.

"There's a form letter here from NASA establishing the ground rules for this year's budget and a personal letter from Ted Wartinian saying that conditions are really tight and some cuts look inevitable. In fact, he says there's a possibility the Project might be scrubbed."

Lily glanced at him. "Not a chance," MacDonald said confidently.

"There's a few applications for employment. Not as many as we used to get. The letters from school children I answered myself. And there's the usual nut letters from people who've been receiving messages from outer space, and from one who's had a ride in a UFO. That's what he called it—not a saucer or anything. A feature writer wants to interview you and some others for an article on the Project. I think he's with us. And another one who sounds as if he wants to do an exposé."

MacDonald listened patiently. Lily was a wonder. She could handle everything in the office as well as he could. In fact, things might run smoother if he were not around to take up her time.

"They've both sent some questions for you to answer. And Joe wants to talk to you."

"Joe?"

"One of the janitors."

"What does he want? They couldn't afford to lose a janitor. Good janitors were harder to find than astronomers, harder even than electronicians.

"He says he has to talk to you, but I've heard from some of the lunchroom staff that he's been complaining about getting messages on his—on his—"

"Yes?"

"On his false tooth."

MacDonald sighed. "Pacify him somehow, will you, Lily? If I talk to him we might lose a janitor."

"I'll do my best. And Mrs. MacDonald called. Said it wasn't important and you needn't call back."

"Call her," MacDonald said. "And, Lily—you're coming to the party tomorrow night, aren't you?"

"What would I be doing at a party with all the brains?"

"We want you to come. Maria asked particularly. It isn't all shop talk, you know. And there are never enough women. You might strike it off with one of the young bachelors."

"At my age, Mr. MacDonald? You're just trying to get rid of me."

"Never."

"I'll get Mrs. MacDonald." Lily turned at the door. "I'll think about the party."

MacDonald shuffled through the papers. Down at the bottom was the only one he was interested in—the computer analysis of last night's listening. But he kept it there, on the bottom, as a reward for going through the others. Ted was really worried. *Move over, Ted.* And then the writers. He supposed he would have to work them in somehow. At least it was part of the fallout to locating the Project in Puerto Rico. Nobody just dropped in. And the questions. Two of them caught his attention.

How did you come to be named Project Director? That was the friendly one. *What are your qualifications to be Director?* That was the other. How would he answer them? Could he answer them at all?

Finally he reached the computer analysis, and it was just like those for the rest of the week, and the week before that, and the months and the years before that. No significant correlations. Noise. There were a few peaks of reception—at the twenty-one-centimeter line, for instance—but these were merely concentrated noise. Radiating clouds of hydrogen, as the Little Ear functioned like an ordinary radio telescope.

At least the Project showed some results. It was feeding star survey data tapes into the international pool. Fallout. Of a process that had no other product except negatives.

Maybe the equipment wasn't sensitive enough. Maybe. They could beef it up some more. At least it might be a successful ploy with the Committee, some progress to present, if only in the hardware. You don't stand still. You spend more money or they cut you back—or off.

Note: Saunders—plans to increase sensitivity.

Maybe the equipment wasn't discriminating enough. But they had used up a generation of ingenuity canceling out background noise, and in its occasional checks the Big Ear indicated that they were doing adequately on terrestrial noise, at least.

Note: Adams—new discrimination gimmick.

Maybe the computer wasn't recognizing a signal when it had one fed into it. Perhaps it wasn't sophisticated enough to perceive certain subtle relationships. . . . And yet sophisticated codes had been broken in seconds. And the Project was asking it to distinguish only where a signal existed, whether the reception was random noise or had some element of the unrandom. At this level it wasn't even being asked to note the influence of consciousness.

Note: ask computer—is it missing something? Ridiculous? Ask Olsen.

Maybe they shouldn't be searching the radio spectrum at all. Maybe radio was a peculiarity of man's civilization. Maybe others had never had it or had passed it by and now had more sophisticated means of communication. Lasers, for instance. Telepathy, or what might pass for it with man. Maybe gamma rays, as Morrison suggested years before Ozma.

Well, maybe. But if it were so, somebody else would have to listen for those. He had neither the equipment nor the background nor the working lifetime left to tackle something new.

And maybe Adams was right.

He buzzed Lily. "Have you reached Mrs. MacDonald?"

"The telephone hasn't answered—"

Unreasoned panic. . . .

"—oh, here she is now. Mr. MacDonald, Mrs. Mac-Donald."

"Hello, darling. I was alarmed when you didn't answer." That had been foolish, he thought, and even more foolish to mention it.

Her voice was sleepy. "I must have been dozing." Even drowsy, it was an exciting voice, gentle, a little husky, that speeded MacDonald's pulse. "What did you want?"

"You called me," MacDonald said.

"Did I? I've forgotten."

"Glad you're resting. You didn't sleep well last night."

"I took some pills."

"How many?"

"Just the two you left out."

"Good girl. I'll see you in a couple of hours. Go back to sleep. Sorry I woke you."

But her voice wasn't sleepy any more. "You won't have to go back tonight, will you? We'll have the evening together?"

"We'll see," he promised.

But he knew he would have to return.

MacDonald paused outside the long, low concrete building which housed the offices and laboratories and computers. It was twilight. The sun had descended below the green hills, but orange and purpling wisps of cirrus trailed down the western sky.

Between MacDonald and the sky was a giant dish held aloft by skeleton metal fingers—held high as if to catch the star dust that drifted down at night from the Milky Way.

> Go and catch a falling star,
>   Get with child a mandrake root,
> Tell me where all past years are,
>   Or who cleft the Devil's foot;
> Teach me to hear mermaids singing,
>   Or to keep off envy's stinging,
>   And find
>   What wind
> Serves to advance an honest mind.

Then the dish began to turn, noiselessly, incredibly, and to tip. And it was not a dish any more but an ear, a listening ear cupped by the surrounding hills to overhear the whispering universe.

Perhaps this was what kept them at their jobs, MacDonald thought. In spite of all disappointments, in spite of all vain efforts, perhaps it was this massive machinery, as sensitive as their fingertips, which kept them struggling with the unfathomable. When they grew weary at their electronic listening posts, when their eyes grew dim with looking at unrevealing dials and studying uneventful graphs, they could step outside their concrete cells and renew their dull spirits in communion with the giant mechanism they commanded, the silent, sensing instrument in which the smallest packets of energy, the smallest waves of matter, were detected in their headlong, eternal flight across the universe. It was the stethoscope with which they took the pulse of the all and noted the birth and death of stars, the probe with which, here on an insignificant planet of an undistinguished star on the edge of its galaxy, they explored the infinite.

Or perhaps it was not just the reality but the imagery,

like poetry, which soothed their doubting souls, the bowl held up to catch Donne's falling star, the ear cocked to catch the suspected shout that faded to an indistinguishable murmur by the time it reached them. And one thousand miles above them was the giant, five-mile-in-diameter network, the largest radio telescope ever built, which men had cast into the heavens to catch the stars.

If they had the Big Ear for more than an occasional reference check, MacDonald thought practically, then they might get some results. But he knew the radio astronomers would never relinquish time to the frivolity of listening for signals that never came. It was only because of the Big Ear that the Project had inherited the Little Ear. There had been talk recently about a larger net, twenty miles in diameter. Perhaps when it was done, if it were done, the Project might inherit time on the Big Ear.

If they could endure until then, MacDonald thought, if they could steer their fragile vessel of faith between the Scylla of self-doubt and the Charybdis of Congressional appropriations.

The images were not all favorable. There were others that went boomp in the night. There was the image, for instance, of man listening, listening, listening to the silent stars, listening for an eternity, listening for signals that would never come, because—the ultimate horror—man was alone in the universe, a cosmic accident of self-awareness which needed and would never receive the comfort of companionship. To be alone, to be all alone, would be like being all alone on earth, with no one to talk to, ever—like being alone inside a bone prison, with no way to get out, no way to communicate with anyone outside, no way to know if anyone was outside. . . .

Perhaps that, in the end, was what kept them going—to stave off the terrors of the night. While they listened there was hope; to give up now would be to admit final defeat. Some said they should never have started; then they never would have the problem of surrender. Some of the new religions said that. The Solitarians, for one. There is nobody there; we are the one, the only created intelligence in the uni-

verse. Let us glory in our uniqueness. But the older religions
encouraged the Project to continue. Why would God have
created the myriads of other stars and other planets if He had
not intended them for living creatures; why should man only
be created in His image? Let us find out, they said. Let us
communicate with them. What revelations have they had?
What saviors have redeemed them?

*These are the words which I spake unto you, while I was
yet with you, that all things must be fulfilled, which were
written in the law of Moses, and in the prophets, and in the
psalms, concerning me. . . . Thus it is written, and thus it
behoved Christ to suffer, and to rise from the dead the third
day: and that repentance and remission of sins should be
preached in his name among all nations, beginning at Jerusalem. And ye are witnesses of these things.*

*And, behold, I send the promise of my Father upon you:
but tarry ye in the city of Jerusalem, until ye be endued with
power from on high.*

Dusk had turned to night. The sky had turned to black.
The stars had been born again. The listening had begun.
MacDonald made his way to his car in the parking lot behind
the building, coasted until he was behind the hill, and turned
on the motor for the long drive home.

The hacienda was dark. It had that empty feeling about it
that MacDonald knew so well, the feeling it had for him
when Maria went to visit friends in Mexico City. But it was
not empty now. Maria was here.

He opened the door and flicked on the hall light. "Maria?"
He walked down the tiled hall, not too fast, not too slow.
"¿Querida?" He turned on the living room light as he passed.
He continued down the hall, past the dining room, the guest
room, the study, the kitchen. He reached the dark doorway to
the bedroom. "Maria Chavez?"

He turned on the bedroom light, low. She was asleep,
her face peaceful, her dark hair scattered across the pillow. She lay on her side, her legs drawn up under the
covers.

Men che dramma
Di sangue m'e rimaso, che no tremi;
Conosco i segni dell' antica fiamma.

MacDonald looked down at her, comparing her features one by one with those he had fixed in his memory. Even now, with those dark, expressive eyes closed, she was the most beautiful woman he had ever seen. What glories they had known! He renewed his spirit in the warmth of his remembrances, recalling moments with loving details.

C'est de quoy j'ay le plus de peur que la peur.

He sat down upon the edge of the bed and leaned over to kiss her upon the cheek and then upon her upthrust shoulder where the gown had slipped down. She did not waken. He shook her shoulder gently. "Maria!" She turned upon her back, straightening. She sighed, and her eyes came open, staring blankly. "It is Robby," MacDonald said, dropping unconsciously into a faint brogue.

Her eyes came alive and her lips smiled sleepily. "Robby. You're home."

"*Yo te amo,*" he murmured, and kissed her. As he pulled himself away, he said, "I'll start dinner. Wake up and get dressed. I'll see you in half an hour. Or sooner."

"Sooner," she said.

He turned and went to the kitchen. There was romaine lettuce in the refrigerator, and as he rummaged further, some thin slices of veal. He prepared Caesar salad and veal scallopine, doing it all quickly, expertly. He liked to cook. The salad was ready, and the lemon juice, tarragon, white wine, and a minute later, the beef bouillon had been added to the browned veal when Maria appeared.

She stood in the doorway, slim, lithe, lovely, and sniffed the air. "I smell something delicious."

It was a joke. When Maria cooked, she cooked Mexican, something peppery that burned all the way into the stomach and lay there like a banked furnace. When MacDonald cooked, it was something exotic—French, perhaps, or Italian, or Chinese. But whoever cooked, the other had to appreciate it or take over all the cooking for a week.

MacDonald filled their wine glasses. "*A la très-bonne, à la très-belle,*" he said, "*qui fait ma joie et ma santé.*"

"To the Project," Maria said. "May there be a signal received tonight."

MacDonald shook his head. One should not mention what one desires too much. "Tonight there is only us."

Afterward there were only the two of them, as there had been now for twenty years. And she was as alive and as urgent, as filled with love and laughter, as when they first had been together.

At last the urgency was replaced by a vast ease and contentment in which for a time the thought of the Project faded into something remote, which one day he would return to and finish. "Maria," he said.

"Robby?"

"*Yo te amo, corazón.*"

"*Yo te amo,* Robby."

Gradually then, as he waited beside her for her breathing to slow, the Project returned. When he thought she was asleep, he got up and began to dress in the dark.

"Robby?" Her voice was awake and frightened.

"*¿Querida?*"

"You are going again?"

"I didn't want to wake you."

"Do you have to go?"

"It's my job."

"Just this once. Stay with me tonight."

He turned on the light. In the dimness he could see that her face was concerned but not hysterical. "*Rast ich, so rost ich.* Besides, I would feel ashamed."

"I understand. Go, then. Come home soon."

He put out two pills on the little shelf in the bathroom and put the others away again.

The headquarters building was busiest at night when the radio noise of the sun was least and listening to the stars was best. Girls bustled down the halls with coffee pots, and men stood near the water fountain, talking earnestly.

MacDonald went into the control room. Adams was at the control panel; Montaleone was the technician. Adams looked up, pointed to his earphones with a gesture of futility, and shrugged. MacDonald nodded at him, nodded at Montaleone, and glanced at the graph. It looked random to him.

Adams leaned past him to point out a couple of peaks. "These might be something." He had removed the earphones.

"Odds," MacDonald said.

"Suppose you're right. The computer hasn't sounded any alarms."

"After a few years of looking at these things, you get the feel of them. You begin to think like a computer."

"Or you get oppressed by failure."

"There's that."

The room was shiny and efficient, glass and metal and plastic, all smooth and sterile; and it smelled like electricity. MacDonald knew that electricity had no smell, but that was the way he thought of it. Perhaps it was the ozone that smelled or warm insulation or oil. Whatever it was, it wasn't worth the time to find out, and MacDonald didn't really want to know. He would rather think of it as the smell of electricity. Perhaps that was why he was a failure as a scientist. "A scientist is a man who wants to know why," his teachers always had told him

MacDonald leaned over the control panel and flicked a switch. A thin, hissing noise filled the room. It was something like air escaping from an inner tube—a susurration of surreptitious sibilants from subterranean sessions of seething serpents.

He turned a knob and the sound became what someone— Tennyson?—had called "the murmuring of innumerable bees." Again, and it became Matthew Arnold's

> . . . melancholy, long withdrawing roar
> Retreating, to the breath
> Of the night wind, down the vast edges drear
> And naked shingles of the world.

He turned the knob once more, and the sound was a babble of distant voices, some shouting, some screaming, some conversing calmly, some whispering—all of them trying beyond desperation to communicate, and everything just below the level of intelligibility. If he closed his eyes, MacDonald could almost see their faces, pressed against a distant screen, distorted with the awful effort to make themselves heard and understood.

But they all insisted on speaking at once. MacDonald wanted to shout at them. "Silence, everybody! All but you—there, with the purple antenna. One at a time and we'll listen to all of you if it takes a hundred years or a hundred lifetimes."

"Sometimes," Adams said, "I think it was a mistake to put in the speaker system. You begin to anthropomorphize. After a while you begin to hear things. Sometimes you even get messages. I don't listen to the voices any more. I used to wake up in the night with someone whispering to me. I was just on the verge of getting the message that would solve everything, and I would wake up." He flicked off the switch.

"Maybe someday somebody will get the message," MacDonald said. "That's what the audio frequency translation is intended to do. To keep the attention focused. It can mesmerize and it can torment, but these are the conditions out of which spring inspiration."

"Also madness," Adams said. "You've got to be able to continue."

"Yes." MacDonald picked up the earphones Adams had put down and held one of them to his ear.

"Tico-tico, tico-tico," it sang. "They're listening in Puerto Rico. Listening for words that never come. Tico-tico, ticotico. They're listening in Puerto Rico. Can it be the stars are stricken dumb?"

MacDonald put the earphones down and smiled. "Maybe there's inspiration in that, too."

"At least it takes my mind off the futility."

"Maybe off the job, too? Do you really want to find anyone out there?"

"Why else would I be here? But there are times when I wonder if we would not be better off not knowing."

"We all think that sometimes," MacDonald said.

In his office he attacked the stack of papers and letters again. When he had worked his way to the bottom, he sighed and got up, stretching. He wondered if he would feel better, less frustrated, less uncertain, if he were working on the Problem instead of just working so somebody else could work on the Problem. But somebody had to do it. Somebody had to keep the Project going, personnel coming in, funds in the bank, bills paid, feathers smoothed.

Maybe it was more important that he do all the dirty little work in the office. Of course it was routine. Of course Lily could do it as well as he. But it was important that he do it, that there be somebody in charge who believed in the Project —or who never let his doubts be known.

Like the Little Ear, he was a symbol—and it is by symbols men live—or refuse to let their despair overwhelm them.

The janitor was waiting for him in the outer office.

"Can I see you, Mr. MacDonald?" the janitor said.

"Of course, Joe," MacDonald said, locking the door of his office carefully behind him. "What is it?"

"It's my teeth, sir." The old man got to his feet and with a deft movement of his tongue and mouth dropped his teeth into his hand.

MacDonald stared at them with a twinge of revulsion. There was nothing wrong with them. They were a carefully constructed pair of false teeth, but they looked too real. MacDonald always had shuddered away from those things which seemed to be what they were not, as if there were some treachery in them.

"They talk to me, Mr. MacDonald," the janitor mumbled, staring at the teeth in his hand with what seemed like suspicion. "In the glass beside my bed at night, they whisper to me. About things far off, like. Messages, like."

MacDonald stared at the janitor. It was a strange word for the old man to use, and hard to say without teeth. Still, the word had been "messages." But why should it be strange? He could have picked it up around the offices or the laboratories. It would be odd, indeed, if he had not picked up something about what was going on. Of course: messages.

"I've heard of that sort of thing happening," MacDonald said. "False teeth accidentally constructed into a kind of crystal set, that pick up radio waves. Particularly near a powerful station. And we have a lot of stray frequencies floating around, what with the antennas and all. Tell you what, Joe. We'll make an appointment with the Project dentist to fix your teeth so that they don't bother you. Any small alteration should do it."

"Thank you, Mr. MacDonald," the old man said. He fitted his teeth back into his mouth. "You're a great man, Mr. Mac-Donald."

MacDonald drove the ten dark miles to the hacienda with a vague feeling of unease, as if he had done something during the day or left something undone that should have been otherwise.

But the house was dark when he drove up in front, not empty-dark as it had seemed to him a few hours before, but friendly-dark. Maria was asleep, breathing peacefully.

The house was brilliant with lighted windows that cast long fingers into the night, probing the dark hills, and the sound of many voices stirred echoes until the countryside itself seemed alive.

"Come in, Lily," MacDonald said at the door, and was reminded of a winter scene when a Lily had met the gentle-men at the door and helped them off with their overcoats. But that was another Lily and another occasion and another place and somebody else's imagination. "I'm glad you decided to come." He had a can of beer in his hand, and he waved it in the general direction of the major center of noisemaking. "There's beer in the living room and something more potent in the study—190 proof grain alcohol, to be precise. Be care-ful with that. It will sneak up on you. But—*nunc est biben-dum!*"

"Where's Mrs. MacDonald?" Lily asked.

"Back there, somewhere." MacDonald waved again. "The men, and a few brave women, are in the study. The women, and a few brave men are in the living room. The kitchen is common territory. Take your choice."

"I really shouldn't have come," Lily said. "I offered to spell Mr. Saunders in the control room, but he said I hadn't been checked out. It isn't as if the computer couldn't handle it all alone, and I know enough to call somebody if anything unexpected should happen."

"Shall I tell you something, Lily?" MacDonald said. "The computer could do it alone. And you and the computer could do it better than any of us, including me. But if the men ever feel that they are unnecessary, they would feel more useless than ever. They would give up. And they mustn't do that."

"Oh, Mac!" Lily said.

"They mustn't do that. Because one of them is going to come up with the inspiration that solves it all. Not me. One of them. We'll send somebody to relieve Charley before the evening is over."

Wer immer strebens sich bemüht,
Den konnen wir erlösen.

Lily sighed. "Okay, boss."

"And enjoy yourself!"

"Okay, boss, okay."

"Find a man, Lily," MacDonald muttered. And then he, too, turned toward the living room, for Lily had been the last who might come.

He listened for a moment at the doorway, sipping slowly from the warming can.

"—work more on gamma rays—"

"Who's got the money to build a generator? Since nobody's built one yet, we don't even know what it might cost."

"—gamma-ray sources should be a million times more rare than radio sources at twenty-one centimeters—"

"That's what Cocconi said nearly fifty years ago. The same arguments. Always the same arguments."

"If they're right, they're right."

"But the hydrogen-emission line is so uniquely logical. As Morrison said to Cocconi—and Cocconi, if you remember, agreed—it represents a logical, prearranged rendezvous point. 'A unique, objective standard of frequency, which must be known to every observer of the universe,' was the way they put it."

"—but the noise level—"

MacDonald smiled and moved on to the kitchen for a cold can of beer.

"—Bracewell's 'automated messengers'?" a voice asked

querulously.

"What about them?"

"Why aren't we looking for them?"

"The point of Bracewell's messengers is that they make themselves known to us!"

"Maybe there's something wrong with ours. After a few million years in orbit—"

"—laser beams make more sense."

"And get lost in all that star shine?"

"As Schwartz and Townes pointed out, all you have to do is select a wave length of light that is absorbed by stellar atmospheres. Put a narrow laser beam in the center of one of the calcium absorption lines—"

In the study they were talking about quantum noise.

"Quantum noise favors low frequencies."

"But the noise itself sets a lower limit on those frequencies."

"Drake calculated the most favorable frequencies, considering the noise level, lie between 3.2 and 8.1 centimeters."

"Drake! Drake! What did he know? We've had nearly fifty years experience on him. Fifty years of technological advance. Fifty years ago we could send radio messages one thousand light-years and laser signals ten light-years. Today those figures are ten thousand and five hundred at least."

"What if nobody's there?" Adams said gloomily.

Ich bin der Geist der stets verneint.

"Short-pulse it, like Oliver suggested. One hundred million billion watts in a ten billionth of a second would smear across the entire radio spectrum. Here, Mac, fill this, will you?"

And MacDonald wandered away through the clustering guests toward the bar.

"And I told Charley," said a woman to two other women in the corner, "if I had a dime for every dirty diaper I've changed, I sure wouldn't be sitting here in Puerto Rico—"

"—neutrinos," said somebody.

"Nuts," said somebody else, as MacDonald poured grain alcohol carefully into the glass and filled it with orange juice, "the only really logical medium is Q waves."

"I know—the waves we haven't discovered yet but are going to discover about ten years from now. Only here it is nearly fifty years after Morrison suggested it, and we still haven't discovered them."

MacDonald wended his way back across the room.

"It's the night work that gets me," said someone's wife. "The kids up all day, and then he wants me there to greet him when he gets home at dawn. Brother!"

"Or what if everybody's listening?" Adams said gloomily. "Maybe everybody's sitting there, listening, just the way we are, because it's so much cheaper than sending."

"Here you are," MacDonald said.

"But don't you suppose somebody would have thought of that by this time and begun to send?"

"Double-think it all the way through and figure what just occurred to you would have occurred to everybody else, so you might as well listen. Think about it—everybody sitting around, listening. If there is anybody. Either way it makes the skin creep."

"All right, then, we ought to send something."

"What would you send?"

"I'd have to think about it. Prime numbers, maybe."

"Think some more. What if a civilization weren't mathematical?"

"Idiot! How would they build an antenna?"

"Maybe they'd rule-of-thumb it, like a ham. Or maybe they have built-in antennae."

"And maybe you have built-in antennae and don't know it."

MacDonald's can of beer was empty. He wandered back toward the kitchen again.

"—insist on equal time with the Big Ear. Even if nobody's sending we could pick up the normal electronic commerce of a civilization tens of light-years away. The problem would be deciphering, not hearing."

"They're picking it up now, when they're studying the relatively close systems. Ask for a tape and work out your program."

"All right, I will. Just give me a chance to work up a

request—"

MacDonald found himself beside Maria. He put his arm around her waist and pulled her close. "All right?" he said.

"All right."

Her face was tired, though, MacDonald thought. He dreaded the notion that she might be growing older, that she was entering middle age. He could face it for himself. He could feel the years piling up inside his bones. He still thought of himself, inside, as twenty, but he knew that he was forty-seven, and mostly he was glad that he had found happiness and love and peace and serenity. He even was willing to pay the price in youthful exuberance and belief in his personal immortality. But not Maria!

> *Nel mezzo del cammin di nostra vita*
> *Mi ritrovai per una selva oscura,*
> *Che la diritta via era smarrita.*

"Sure?"

She nodded.

He leaned close to her ear. "I wish it was just the two of us, as usual."

"I, too."

"I'm going to leave in a little while—"

"Must you?"

"I must relieve Saunders. He's on duty. Give him an opportunity to celebrate a little with the others."

"Can't you send somebody else?"

"Who?" MacDonald gestured with good-humored futility at all the clusters of people held together by bonds of ordered sounds shared consecutively. "It's a good party. No one will miss me."

"I will."

"Of course, *querida.*"

"You are their mother, father, priest, all in one," Maria said. "You worry about them too much."

"I must keep them together. What else am I good for?"

"For much more."

MacDonald hugged her with one arm.

"Look at Mac and Maria, will you?" said someone who was having trouble with his consonants. "What god-damned devotion!''

MacDonald smiled and suffered himself to be pounded on the back while he protected Maria in front of him. "I'll see you later," he said.

As he passed the living room someone was saying, "Like Eddie said, we ought to look at the long-chain molecules in carbonaceous chondrites. No telling how far they've traveled —or been sent—or what messages might be coded in the molecules."

As he closed the front door behind him, the noise dropped to a roar and then a mutter. He stopped for a moment at the door of the car and looked up at the sky.

E quindi uscimmo a riveder le stelle.

The noise from the hacienda reminded him of something —the speakers in the control room. All those voices talking, talking, talking, and from here he could not understand a thing.

Somewhere there was an idea if he could only concentrate on it hard enough. But he had drunk one beer too many—or perhaps one too few.

After the long hours of listening to the voices, MacDonald always felt a little crazy, but tonight it was worse than usual. Perhaps it was all the conversation before, or the beers, or something else—some deeper concern that would not surface.

But then the listeners had to be crazy to begin with—to get committed to a project that might go for centuries without results.

Tico-tico, tico-tico. . . .

Even if they could pick up a message, they still would likely be dead and gone before any exchange could take place even with the nearest likely star. What kind of mad dedication could sustain such perseverance?

They're listening in Puerto Rico. . . .

Religion could. At least once it did, during the era of cathedral building in Europe, the cathedrals that took centuries to build.

"What are you doing, fellow?"

"I'm working for ten francs a day."

"And what are you doing?"

"I'm laying stone."

"And you—what are you doing?"

"I am building a cathedral."

They were building cathedrals, most of them. Most of them had that religious mania about their mission that would sustain them through a lifetime of labors in which no progress could be seen.

Listening for words that never come. . . .

The mere layers of stone and those who worked for pay alone eliminated themselves in time and left only those who kept alive in themselves the concept, the dream.

But they had to be a little mad to begin with.

Can it be the stars are stricken dumb?

Tonight he had heard the voices nearly all night long. They kept trying to tell him something, something urgent, something he should do, but he could not quite make out the words. There was only the babble of distant voices, urgent and unintelligible.

Tico-tico, tico-tic. . . .

He had wanted to shout "Shut up!" to the universe. "One at a time!" "You first!" But of course there was no way to do that. Or had he tried? Had he shouted?

They're listening with ears this big!

Had he dozed at the console with the voices mumbling in his ears, or had he only thought he dozed? Or had he only dreamed he waked. Or dreamed he dreamed?

Listening for thoughts just like their own.

There was a madness to it all, but perhaps it was a divine madness, a creative madness. And is not that madness that which sustains man in his terrible self-knowledge, the driving madness which demands reason of a casual universe, the awful aloneness which seeks among the stars for companionship?

Can it be that we are all alone?

The ringing of the telephone half-penetrated through the mists of mesmerization. He picked up the handset, half-expecting that it would be the universe calling, perhaps with a clipped British accent, "Hello there, Man. Hello. Hello. I say, we seem to have a bad connection, what? Just wanted you to know that we're here. Are you there? Are you listening? Message on the way. May not get there for a couple of centuries. Do be around to answer, will you? That's a good being. Righto. . . ."

Only it wasn't. It was the familiar American voice of Charley Saunders saying, "Mac, there's been an accident. Olsen is on his way to relieve you, but I think you'd better leave now. It's Maria."

Leave it. Leave it all. What does it matter? But leave the controls on automatic; the computer can take care of it all. Maria! Get in the car. Start it. Don't fumble! That's it. Go. Go. Car passing. Must be Olsen. No matter.

What kind of accident? Why didn't I ask? What does it matter what kind of accident? Maria. Nothing could have happened. Nothing serious. Not with all those people around. *Nil desperandum.* And yet why did Charley call if it was not serious? Must be serious. I must be prepared for something bad, something that will shake the world, that will tear my insides.

I must not break up in front of them. Why not? Why must I appear infallible? Why must I always be cheerful, imperturbable, my faith unshaken? Why me? If there is something bad, if something impossibly bad has happened to Maria, what will matter? Ever? Why didn't I ask Charley what it was? Why? The bad can wait; it will get no worse for being unknown.

What does the universe care for my agony? I am nothing. My feelings are nothing to anyone but me. My only possible meaning to the universe is the Project. Only this slim potential links me with eternity. My love and my agony are me, but the significance of my life or death are the Project.

HIC.SITVS.EST.PHAETHON.CVRRVS.AVRIGA.PATERNI
QVEM.SI.NON.TENVIT.MAGNIS.TAMEN.EXCIDIT.AVSIS

By the time he reached the hacienda, MacDonald was breathing evenly. His emotions were under control. Dawn had grayed the eastern sky. It was a customary hour for Project personnel to be returning home.

Saunders met him at the door. "Dr. Lessenden is here. He's with Maria."

The odor of stale smoke and the memory of babble still lingered in the air, but someone had been busy. The party remains had been cleaned up. No doubt they all had pitched in. They were good people.

"Betty found her in the bathroom off your bedroom. She wouldn't have been there except the others were occupied. I blame myself. I shouldn't have let you relieve me. Maybe if you had been here—But I knew you wanted it that way."

"No one's to blame. She was alone a great deal," MacDonald said. "What happened?"

"Didn't I tell you? Her wrists. Slashed with a razor. Both of them. Betty found her in the bathtub. Like pink lemonade, she said."

Percé jusques au fond du coeur
D'une atteinte imprévue aussi bien que mortelle.

A fist tightened inside MacDonald's gut and then slowly relaxed. Yes, it had been that. He had known it, hadn't he? He had known it would happen ever since the sleeping pills, even though he had kept telling himself, as she had told him, that the overdose had been an accident.

Or had he known? He knew only that Saunders's news had been no surprise.

Then they were at the bedroom door, and Maria was lying under a blanket on the bed, scarcely making it mound over her body; and her arms were on top of the blankets, palms up, bandages like white paint across the olive perfection of her arms, now, MacDonald reminded himself, no longer perfection, but marred with ugly red lips that spoke to him of hidden misery and untold sorrow and a life that was a lie. . . .

Dr. Lessenden looked up, sweat trickling down from his hairline. "The bleeding is stopped, but she's lost a good deal of blood. I've got to take her to the hospital for a transfusion. The ambulance should be here any minute." He paused. MacDonald looked at Maria's face. It was paler than he had ever seen it. It looked almost waxen, as if it were already arranged for all time on a satin pillow. "Her chances are fifty-fifty," Lessenden said in answer to his unspoken question.

And then the attendants brushed their way past him with their litter.

"Betty found this on her dressing table," Saunders said. He handed MacDonald a slip of paper folded once.

MacDonald unfolded it: *Je m'en vay chercher un grand Peut-être.*

Everyone was surprised to see MacDonald at the office. They did not say anything, and he did not volunteer the information that he could not bear to sit at home, among the remembrances, and wait for word to come. But they asked him about Maria, and he said, "Dr. Lessenden is hopeful. She's still unconscious. Apparently will be for some time. The doctor said I might as well wait here as at the hospital. I think I made them nervous. They're hopeful. Maria's still unconscious. . . ."

O lente, lente currite, noctis equi!
The stars move still, time runs, the clock will strike. . . .

Finally MacDonald was alone. He pulled out paper and pencil and worked for a long time on the statement, and then he balled it up and threw it into the wastebasket, scribbled a single sentence on another sheet of paper, and called Lily.

"Send this!"

She glanced at it. "No, Mac."

"Send it!"

"But—"

"It's not an impulse. I've thought it over carefully. Send it."

Slowly she left, holding the piece of paper gingerly in her fingertips. MacDonald pushed the papers around on his desk, waiting for the telephone to ring. But without knocking, unannounced, Saunders came through the door first.

"You can't do this, Mac," Saunders said.

MacDonald sighed. "Lily told you. I would fire that girl if she weren't so loyal."

"Of course she told me. This isn't just you. It affects the whole Project."

"That's what I'm thinking about."

"I think I know what you're going through, Mac—" Saunders stopped. "No, of course I don't know what you're going through. It must be hell. But don't desert us. Think of the Project!'"

"That's what I'm thinking about. I'm a failure, Charley. Everything I touch—ashes."

"You're the best of us."

"A poor linguist? An indifferent engineer? I have no qualifications for this job, Charley. You need someone with ideas to head the Project, someone dynamic, someone who can lead, someone with—charisma."

A few minutes later he went over it all again with Olsen. When he came to the qualifications part, all Olsen could say was, "You give a good party, Mac."

It was Adams, the skeptic, who affected him most. "Mac, you're what I believe in instead of God."

Sonnenborn said, "You are the Project. If you go, it all falls apart. It's over."

"It seems like it, always, but it never happens to those things that have life in them. The Project was here before I came. It will be here after I leave. It must be longer lived than any of us, because we are for the years and it is for the centuries."

After Sonnenborn, MacDonald told Lily wearily, "No more, Lily."

None of them had had the courage to mention Maria, but MacDonald considered that failure, too. She had tried to communicate with him a month ago when she took the pills, and he had been unable to understand. How could he riddle the stars when he couldn't even understand those closest to him? Now he had to pay.

> *Meine Ruh' ist hin,*
> *Meine Herz ist schwer.*

What would Maria want? He knew what she wanted, but if she lived, he could not let her pay that price. Too long she had been there when he wanted her, waiting like a doll put away on a shelf for him to return and take her down, so that he could have the strength to continue.

And somehow the agony had built up inside her, the dreadful progress of the years, most dread of all to a beautiful woman growing old, alone, too much alone. He had been selfish. He had kept her to himself. He had not wanted chil-

dren to mar the perfection of their being together.
Perfection for him; less than that for her.

Perhaps it was not too late for them if she lived. And if she
died—he would not have the heart to go on with work to
which, he knew now, he could contribute nothing.

Que acredito su ventura,
Morir querdo y vivir loco.

And finally the call came. "She's going to be all right,
Mac," Lessenden said. And after a moment, "Mac, I said—"
"I heard."
"She wants to see you."
"I'll be there."
"She said to give you a message. 'Tell Robby I've been a
little crazy in the head. I'll be better now. That "great per-
haps" looks too certain from here. And tell him not to be
crazy in the head, too.' "

MacDonald put down the telephone and walked through
the doorway and through the outer office, a feeling in his
chest as if it were going to burst. "She's going to be all right,"
he threw over his shoulder at Lily.

"Oh, Mac—"

In the hall, Joe the janitor stopped him. "Mr. MacDonald
—"

MacDonald stopped. "Been to the dentist yet, Joe?"
"No, sir, not yet, but it's not—"
"Don't go. I'd like to put a tape recorder beside your bed
for a while, Joe. Who knows?"
"Thank you, sir. But it's— They say you're leaving, Mr.
MacDonald."
"Somebody else will do it."
"You don't understand. Don't go, Mr. MacDonald!"
"Why not, Joe?"
"You're the one who cares."

MacDonald had been about to move on, but that stopped
him.

Ful wys is he that can himselven knowe!

He turned and went back to the office. "Have you got that
sheet of paper, Lily?"
"Yes, sir."

"Have you sent it?"

"No, sir."

"Bad girl. Give it to me."

He read the sentence on the paper once more: *I have great confidence in the goals and ultimate success of the Project, but for personal reasons I must submit my resignation.*

He studied it for a moment.

Pigmaei gigantum humeris impositi plusquam ipsi gigantes vidant.

And he tore it up.